Arlo

A DADDY FOR SUMMER

HJ WELCH

Arlo
A Daddy For Summer

Copyright © 2024 by HJ Welch

Cover Design by Jo Clement

This book is a work of fiction. Names, places, and incidents are either products of the author's imagination or are used fictitiously. Any resemblance to actual events, locales, or persons, living or dead, is entirely coincidental.

All rights reserved. No part of this book may be used or reproduced in any manner whatsoever without written permission, except in the case of brief quotations embodied in critical articles and reviews.

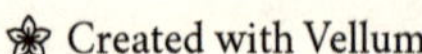 Created with Vellum

Also Available

BY HJ WELCH

Paddle Creek College (Daddies and kink)

#1 Heaven Sent

#2 Yes, Sir

#3 Little Pleasures

#4 Four Play

#5 Hell's Kitten

#6 Make Believe

Pine Cove (Small town)

Complete Box Set

Homecoming Hearts (Former Boy Band)

Complete Box Set

Bears-4-U (Daddies and bears multi-author shared universe)

Keep Me

———

BY HELEN JULIET

Contemporary Fairy Tale Adaptations

The Fairy Tale Collection (Beauty and the Beast, Cinderella, Rapunzel)

Daddy's Fairy Tales (Daddies and kink – Goldilocks, Little Red Riding Hood, The Three Little Pigs, Puss in Boots)

Sweet Tooth (Christmas – Hansel and Gretel)

Jacked Up (D/s – Jack and the Beanstalk)

CHAPTER 1

Thomas

I ALMOST CHANGE MY MIND ABOUT THIS TRIP AT LEAST TEN times on my way to the airport. Even after my bags have been checked and I've made it through security and passport control, I'm still wrestling with myself.

Am I making a huge mistake? Is this going to come back and bite me in the ass in ways I can't possibly imagine right now?

Looking around the private lounge area of Heathrow in London, I sip my can of cola and remind myself that literally no one here knows my intended destination. Hell, I doubt anyone knows who I even *am*. Hockey isn't so big here.

There won't be anything stopping me from changing my mind once I land in Bali, and that thought soothes me. Unless I want to create a scene, I'll soon be getting on that plane regardless. But if I really don't think it'll be worth the risk, I can just cancel my reservation and book somewhere else. Sitting on a beach for ten days will still be very much appreciated, even if it wasn't what I had in mind.

Relieved, I exhale and also remind myself that I'm not doing a damn thing wrong. Simply private. I was lucky enough to have had a strong support network to come out as gay when I was still playing pro. Now that I'm retired, it's even less of an issue. In fact, the internet seems desperate for me to find a boyfriend.

The issue is keeping the kind of boyfriend I want behind closed doors. People are mean and opinionated. There's a high chance they won't understand that what I want is perfectly fine between consenting adults.

More than fine. God, I *yearn* for it.

After my knee got blown out in a matter of seconds and ended my career, I was rich enough that I could have never worked again, even though I was only thirty-five. That's not in my nature, though. Besides, Mama and Abuela raised me better than to sit around on my ass. So I threw myself into helping others by creating a foundation for under privileged kids to learn to play hockey, and then I set up several college scholarships in my name.

In doing all that, I discovered the thing that gives me even *more* joy and fulfillment than being out on the ice.

Helping people. Caring for people.

That's what I want in a boyfriend.

Yeah, yeah. I'm sure there are a lot of sweet guys out there who would enjoy being doted on, but I'm not talking about a sugar baby. I want a baby *boy*.

It's something I've only read about until now, but I've imagined it vividly for years. I want someone to call me Daddy and let me make sure he always has someone in his corner helping him with whatever he needs. Someone who enjoys letting all their cares go when they become their littlest self.

That's where the court of public opinion gets blurry, and it scares the hell out of me that one wrong move with the wrong person could undo everything I've achieved in both of my careers. I help kids. Kids look up to me. This is completely separate from that, but some people might not see it that way.

I take another breath and finish off my soda. That's why going to a specifically kinky retreat is a *good* idea. Everyone there will be like-minded, and if I keep my sunglasses and baseball cap on and go by just 'Tom' instead of my full name, with any luck, no one should recognize my true identity.

It's worth the risk if I can just let go of my fears. I have everything I want in life—loving family, friends, fans, money, a new career I love. Is it too much to hope for a relationship as well?

Maybe. But if I don't start trying, I'll never know. As I approach turning forty, this seems like the right time to get myself in the game. Fortunately, getting older goes in my favor. That's what a lot of people expect in a Daddy. But honestly? I don't care what age my boy is. Just so long as he lets me dote on him. I think that—

"Is this seat taken?"

I blink myself out of my reverie and focus on the young man in front of me who is pointing at the armchair I didn't even notice had become vacated. His accent is astonishingly posh, even for a Brit. In many ways, he's quite unremarkable. Early to mid-twenties. Brown hair that just curls around his ears and a little scruff on his chin. Medium height and weight, wearing a light-blue Henley and dark jeans.

But the way his eyes *sparkle* makes my breath catch, if only for a second. I blink again, shaking my head as I remember what he asked.

"Oh, yeah," I say, wincing at my Brooklyn accent that sounds nasally to my ears in that moment. "The lady who was there took all her stuff, so I assume you're good to go."

"Thank you ever so much," he says with a beaming smile. Wow, he really sounds like he should be on one of those historical TV shows with all the ballgowns and hand fans that my big sister goes nuts for.

He drops into the seat and excitedly gets wireless headphones out of his backpack. Once they're settled on his head and he selects whatever he's listening to on his phone, he pulls out a notebook and starts scribbling.

It could be a diary entry. It could be a shopping list. All I know is that it's none of my business, and I need to stop staring at this guy. I try to tear my eyes away, but as I do, I spot a colorful plush parrot keyring on his backpack that makes me smile.

Cute.

As captivating as this young man is, I need to leave him be. He's going on vacation or possibly traveling for work or to visit family. At no point did he consent to being spied on. I guess I've just got romance on the brain. Usually, I don't look twice at adorable guys out in the wild. But something about this boy is absolutely captivating.

Man. Not boy.

Yeah, I need this retreat. I'm going to explode if I don't allow myself the space to express my needs soon. This innocent stranger is making all my Daddy instincts scream, and all he's doing is just sitting down.

To keep my eyes off him, I pull out my phone and start looking through the retreat itinerary options again. There are all kinds of events to cater to different kinds of kink, so I'm not sure how many of them I'll be interested in attending. But they could be illuminating if nothing else.

I'm not into bondage or pain play, but I might learn something. Spanking is probably going to come up if my hypothetical baby boy acts out, and it would be good to understand that better. I hate the idea of hurting someone special to me, but logically I know it can be extremely cathartic. Littles often need boundaries set for them, and it will be my job to guide my boy and help him safely. It sounds daunting, but this is all part of the learning curve I'm hoping for from this retreat.

Whatever the case, I'm always willing to expand my horizons. I'll give anything a go. Saying 'yes' more than 'no' is what's got me this far in my extraordinary life.

The sandcastle competition, pool disco, and finger-painting session, on the other hand, sound just wonderful. If I can find a boy to share them with. Maybe I'll be able to meet one at those events, if not before? There's always hope.

Sensing movement, I glance up and see the adorable young man hurriedly gathering up his things and rushing off. My heart drops, but I'm being ridiculous if I thought I was going to speak to him any further. However, his departure does prompt me to check the display board, and my heart leaps a fraction when I see that my gate has been announced. Excellent.

I also get my belongings together at a more leisurely pace, and as I stand, I give the area a once-over to ensure I haven't forgotten anything. That's when my eye catches something tucked in the corner of the armchair where the cute guy was just sitting.

Oh, no.

Before I even pluck it out, I can see it's a passport. The British one is different from mine, but it's immediately obvious what it is. Worse than that, it's got his boarding pass wedged in between the pages.

Panic grips my chest on his behalf. Will he notice in time? I should give it to a member of staff at the lounge so if he comes back and asks, they'll have it kept safe for him. But leaving such an important task in the hands of a stranger makes me uneasy, so on the off chance his gate is on the way to mine, I check the ticket.

The first thing I notice is his name. Arlington Hythe-

Wandsworth. *Wow.* That sure is something. Then I look for a gate number.

Holy shit.

We're on the same flight? What the hell?

I don't have time to wonder at how small the chances of that happening are. Instead, I slip his documents into my breast pocket and race out of the private lounge, hoping that I don't miss him coming back this way.

Luckily, the gate isn't too far away. Heathrow is an enormous airport, after all. As I approach the waiting area, my second bit of good fortune is clear. There, kneeling on the ground, frantically emptying his bag out, is my young man.

Arlington.

He looks close to tears, and my heart aches. So I waste no time running up to him, already fishing out his passport and the accompanying boarding pass, holding it out as I jog up to him and crouch down.

"You left this in the lounge," I say with a grin, ignoring my protesting knee after such a short sprint. The damn thing can take a back seat for once.

Arlington's eyes go wide as he absorbs the sight of me and what's in my hand. "Oh goodness gracious me!" he cries, snatching the passport before opening it up to verify his ticket is also there. "You absolute gent! I was almost in a proper bother there!" He clutches the documents to his chest and gives me a watery smile like sunshine peeking through the clouds. *"Thank* you."

My heart flips, but I do my best to ignore it. I just need to count my blessings that I got another chance to see this sweet guy, but I realize that it probably doesn't mean anything. "No problem, man. Just make sure you put everything back in that bag so you don't lose anything this time."

Okay…so I couldn't resist the tiniest bit of Daddying. But the way he beams up at me makes it worth it.

"I will, I promise. Thank you ever so much once again!" Damn. The way this kid talks is killing me. It's just too stinking cute.

I hear them calling first class, so with a grimace, I stand and wink down at the young man. "Safe flight."

"You, too," he says earnestly.

It's hard to walk away. I really want to watch over him and make sure that he's got all his stuff safely packed back in the bag. But I've done my good deed for the day. He's got his essential documents in hand, and now our little meet-cute is over.

There's a spring in my step, however. I know it's wrong, but I checked, and he's not getting off in Singapore. He's going all the way to Bali, just like me. That's a lot of hours to be cooped up in a tin can together.

Who knows? Maybe our paths will cross again.

CHAPTER 2

Arlo

Oh, bother. I haven't even gotten on the plane yet, and I almost spoiled everything. My tummy is in knots. But after I've triple-checked everything is in my backpack like it ought to be, I take several deep breaths and join the line to board the plane.

Thank heavens for that dashingly handsome and kind stranger. I get butterflies just thinking about his warm smile. He really chased after me from the lounge. Wow. I bet he'd make a good Daddy.

Ah, no. None of that. I absolutely have to stop pining after random strangers who make me feel good about myself. They can't *all* be Daddies and Mummies. That would be silly.

I can't help wondering where the nice American man went, though. I was so busy with my belongings I didn't see. It's probably for the best. He's most likely off on holiday with his wife…or maybe husband. Who knows? He seemed too gorgeous and responsible to be single.

But what would I know? It's not like I've ever dated. Sex, yes. But a boyfriend? A Daddy?

Only in my dreams, sadly.

I shake myself and pay attention to my surroundings. Daydreaming is how I almost lost my bloody passport and boarding pass in the first place. It's how I get into trouble ninety-nine percent of the time, if I'm being honest. But… blimey. What a truly rotten start to the trip that would have been. It could have ruined everything altogether. I need to be more aware.

This is not new information. I'm painfully aware of how useless I am. Just ask Mummy and Pa.

But they don't know where I'm going. They don't even realize I'm leaving the country. This is my chance at some real, genuine independence. Freedom.

If I can even make it to Bali.

No, I need to stop thinking like that. I'm here, aren't I? And thanks to a very kind (and handsome, did I mention handsome?) stranger, I'm about to get on the plane with everything I need. My suitcase is checked. My transport is booked for the other end. I have everything I could possibly need for a wonderful getaway.

Except a Daddy.

Well, that's why I'm going to this retreat, isn't it? To hopefully find one to practice with for a week or so. I mean, it's difficult to imagine who would be interested in a lost cause like me, but I've always been tragically optimistic, so what can I say?

"Have a nice trip, Mr. …" The nice girl at the desk darts her eyes back to my documents, but I take pity on her.

"Thank you!" I cry cheerfully, plucking my passport back and flashing her a smile. My name is as ridiculous as the family who owns it. I find it best to just ignore it when I can. "You, too!"

You too…what? Have a nice trip?

Oh no.

I bustle down the gangway and remind myself that I'm never going to see the poor lady again as long as I live.

Much like Mr. Handsome-and-Definitely-not-a-Daddy.

I need to get a hold of myself. Just because I've got Daddies on the brain doesn't mean every kind, gorgeous man I meet is eligible. Far from it.

It sounds bad, but well…I'm simply not used to being allowed out of the house. Mingling with common folk is highly unusual for me. I'm just a little excitable.

Like a child on Christmas morning.

As I wait in the queue, hanging in midair inside the rickety-feeling tunnel that connects the building to the plane, I try not to bounce as I think of all the enticing items I have squirreled away in my big suitcase that's tucked somewhere in the belly of this plane. Secret items no one else has ever seen before. Things I've never used before.

Things my father would sneer at me for if he knew about them.

For a second, my smile falters. But then I shake it off, just like my favorite lady, Taylor Swift. My father has no power over me here. None of them do.

I'm free. For ten whole days.

And if I spend that time alone, it will still be an absolute blessing.

I'm pulled from my thoughts by a cheery "Hello!" from the flight attendant waiting inside the threshold of the plane. She checks my ticket and only pauses for a second. "Enjoy your flight," she says, avoiding having to utter my name.

It's not that it's impossible to pronounce. It's just absurd. I'm constantly fighting the urge to reassure people that I hate it too.

"Thank you so much," I say, beaming at her and hoping it'll ease her embarrassment. "You, too!"

Not again.

I mean…how can anyone be embarrassed around me when I do such a fine job of mortifying myself?

At least she actually *is* taking this flight. It's not like when it's my birthday and I happily declare 'You, too' at anyone who sends me wishes on the day. Still, I scurry to my seat and don't look at another soul.

When I booked myself on this excursion, I was feeling all adventurous. Sick of being pandered to, I decided I wanted a taste of 'real life,' so I booked my seat in economy.

We haven't even left the tarmac, and I'm already regretting my decision profusely. The seats are *so* much smaller, and everyone is just so close. I refuse to be a brat about it, however. The fact is that I can't spend all this time loathing my lot in life then turn around and reap all the benefits. It's horribly inevitable that I am the heir to the Hythe-Wandsworth name, fortune, estate, and business.

But if I'm going to be this grumpy about the whole affair, it would be hypocritical to use family money to sneak off on holiday. That's why I've saved every penny for this jaunt by working independently online, editing for several different media outlets. It took a long time, and I've lived in fear of getting found out ever since I started this harebrained scheme. But it was worth it.

I'm here.

Or rather, I'm on my way. And I will just have to put up with the slightly claustrophobic seating arrangements.

My parents think I'm at a conference for young professionals that I've been to before. It's basically an excuse for young men who went to stuffy boarding schools like mine to network, which in reality means half paying attention to generic motivational speeches then drinking excessive amounts of alcohol.

With any luck in the world, my parents will never know the truth. I know Mummy peeks in on my financials, so all

I've got is the extra, secret money I've earned in my new bank account.

It all feels rather daring like I'm a spy or something exciting.

Truthfully, I could be anybody I wanted to be on this trip. I could finally be…Arlo.

It feels sacrilegious to even think the name. But how I've longed to be called that my whole life. Mummy and Pa don't approve of nicknames. They say it's a vulgar, common thing to do to one's birthright. But all throughout school and the rest of my life, I've despised being Arlington. I know it's a highly respectable traditional English name.

But it's also the most famous veterans' cemetery in America, for pity's sake.

Arlo can be whomever he likes. He can be free.

Just not from this seat for the next thirteen hours.

———

There's something freeing about resigning oneself to one's fate. There was nothing to be done about the small seat, the lack of legroom, the passengers around me, or the sheer length of time I was to be confined inside that plane, breathing the same recycled air over and over. I like it when people make decisions for me. It's one of the main reasons I want a Daddy, after all. So I sort of just relax and go with it.

Besides, traveling alone means there's no one around to stop me from watching children's movies. Therefore, I occupy a great deal of my time watching a trilogy about singing unicorns on daring adventures. The cabin crew feeds me several times and are just so friendly and polite. I sleep a little, grateful that I took my cousin's advice and brought a travel pillow.

Ginny is the only one who knows where I'm really going

and why. She's the actual black sheep of the family because she's very out and bisexual and visibly queer with her short black hair, piercings and tattoos. I'm not brave like her. I survive by trying to make myself invisible, but that's quite a lonely way to live.

She's the one who ultimately gave me the courage to do this. I think of how she said she was so proud of me as I doze through the last couple of hours of the flight.

Once we finally land in Singapore, I'm groggy but relieved to fill my lungs with relatively fresh air and stretch out my aching limbs. I've heard that this airport is one of the most incredible ones in the world, with an indoor jungle, butterfly garden, and some kind of artificial waterfall in the middle. Sadly, we're only here for an hour or so while they refuel the plane, so we're basically kept at the gate, and I don't get to see any of that.

It's okay, though. I'm still just as excited that we're so close to Bali now. I've been obsessively looking at photos for months, so it doesn't seem real that I'm almost there. Until we re-plane, I spend my time filling up my water bottle, downing it, using the men's room, and then I just hide away in a corner and stretch some more.

Before I know it, we're being shuffled through passport control and I'm back in my dreaded seat. However, it's only about three hours until we arrive in Bali, so that's not so bad. I've lost all concept of what time it's supposed to be, but I figure getting some extra shut-eye won't hurt me.

I probably only get an hour before the crew wakes us in order to give us some breakfast. I'm not even sure if I'm hungry, but I eat it anyway, especially grateful for the juice and tea after such a long time traveling. I don't want to start off my trip with a dehydration headache.

Even though I'm not next to the window, I eagerly stare outside as the plane makes its final descent onto the tarmac, resisting the urge to cheer as we touch down. *I did it! We're here!*

It's difficult to keep my childish excitement at bay, but *that* part of me is bubbling just below the surface, desperate to come out and play. *Soon,* I tell myself happily as we taxi around. I can feel how anxious everyone around me is to unfasten their seat belts so they can stand up and rescue their carry-on luggage from the overhead lockers. My knees jiggle up and down, and I hug my travel pillow to keep my hands occupied.

Other than almost dropping my bag on my head, I eventually make it off the plane without incident, and finally, I'm on Indonesian soil. It's early in the morning, so the sky looks beautifully hazy as the sun peeks through the clouds. There's air conditioning, but I can still taste how different the air is.

My heart pounds as I struggle to concentrate. This is where I have to do some proper adulting, so I get my notebook out of my backpack and double check all the things I need to tick off my list. I just need to go through passport control and get my bag from luggage claim, then find my car service. After what happened at Heathrow, I added 'PASSPORT AND BOARDING PASS' to remind me to know where they are at all times, both now and on the way back.

It makes my head swim ensuring that I don't do something catastrophic again. But once I get my bottom in a taxi, I'll be done.

I can be Arlo and just let go.

By some miracle, I make it through passport control and pick up my suitcase from the luggage belt in one piece. I don't let myself get distracted by looking at anyone else. Right now, I have to be my own Daddy. I clumsily navigate using the bathroom with all my stuff, but then finally, I'm through to arrivals, and I catch sight of a man with a sign that reads 'Arlo Little.'

My heart skips a beat at my own daring, expecting someone to appear out of nowhere and scream at me that I can't do that. That I'm using a fake name. But of course no one does.

"Hello, yes, that's me," I say breathlessly as I approach the guy and give him a small wave. "Good morning."

My driver's face splits into a big smile. "Good morning, Mr. Little! This way, please."

Before I can protest, he takes the handle of my case and starts wheeling it through the airport. I rush to keep up with him, thinking about how much I need a cup of tea and praying the resort is equipped to deal with displaced Brits needing their hot leaf water. It is five star, after all. I'm sure they accommodate all kinds of people from around the world. I know a lot of the tourists here are Australian, and thanks to their ties with the UK, they have a sensible appreciation of tea as well, or so I'm told.

Gosh, this is the farthest I've ever been from home by far. Mummy and Pa always want to go skiing in Europe. Occasionally, they'd allow me some sun in the south of France, but I think beaches fall into the 'uncouth' category along with so many other things they deem frivolous and I think are just joyful. Who cares if sand is messy? It looks *fun!*

As we step outside the building I am briefly enveloped by warm and humid air. I know it will probably make me sweaty quickly enough, but it feels like a hug to me. I love the way it tastes as I breathe in deeply. We are so far from England now. I'm on a completely different continent, and here's my tangible proof.

As we drive from the airport toward the resort, I stare in awe at the lush vegetation. Tall palm trees wave merrily high above us, and the sunshine streams down. I'm grateful for more air conditioning in the car. There isn't much of that back home, unfortunately.

We largely follow the south coast as we head west, getting closer and closer to where I'm going to call home for the next ten days. It's difficult not to bounce in my seat as I see the sign for Kuta Paradise Resort and Spa and the car makes the turn into the grounds, climbing up the hillside as we go.

"Are you excited, Mr. Little?" my driver asks, looking at me in the rearview mirror. He's grinning like he's in on my secret. I don't hold back for once, finding freedom in confiding in a stranger.

"*So* excited, sir."

His chest puffs out at the honorific. We've barely stopped outside the entrance when he dashes from his seat to open my door for me. Then he produces my case like a magic trick before grabbing my hand to shake it. "Have a wonderful stay, Mr. Little," he says genuinely.

I know tipping isn't expected here or the rest of Asia in general, but that is something my father drilled into me that I appreciate. I used my time during the drive to watch the meter and work out what would be approximately twenty percent by the time we arrived. The currency is a bit confusing because the numbers are enormous compared to what we have back home, but I'm confident I've got it roughly right as I pull the notes from my jeans pocket, where I folded them, and press them into his palm.

"Thank you for getting my holiday off to a lovely start," I tell him with a smile.

"Thank you, Mr. Little," he says breathlessly, glancing down at what I've given him on top of the fare.

Before one of my mortifying quips of 'You, too!' can slip out, I grab my suitcase handle and wheel it confidently through the sliding double doors and into the resort's reception.

The space is huge and airy, with a peaked wooden ceiling and marble floor. Fans spin lazily overhead to keep the cool air moving, and vibrant green plants with an assortment of colorful flowers tumble from pots all over the place. It feels so alive and fresh. I can't stop myself grinning.

And then there are the people. It's a small, high-end resort that a kinky dating app has partnered with to book exclusively for this event. Everyone here for the next ten days will be interested in similar adult pursuits. I see men, women, and people who probably identify in between of all ages milling around. My heartbeat quickens. How many of these men might be Daddies looking to play with a boy?

I'm getting ahead of myself. Besides, loads of people will have already checked in or aren't here yet, so there's no point in trying to set my hopes on anyone right now. But simply knowing that these people are open-minded and that a lot of them will be queer gives me a sense of belonging I've never experienced before in my life. Considering I've never even been brave enough to go to a gay bar for fear of what Mummy and Pa might say or do, it's all a bit overwhelming.

The lady at the desk is an absolute sweetheart, but in my tired and hyper state, I know I'm not giving her my full attention. Especially when someone appears out of nowhere and offers me some sort of delicious fruit smoothie in a coconut shell decorated with a mini umbrella and pretty flowers. I think I might have died and gone to heaven.

I probably say 'thank you' too much and almost certainly slip in a 'you, too!' but really, who cares? I'm here, and it's brilliant, and I simply can't wait to get my swim shorts on so I can go play in the pool. Or *pools*, I should say. From what I can remember, there are three, all with infinity views over the jungle and onto the sea. They fall like waterfalls into the one below. From the photos, it looks like something out of a dream, so I can't imagine what it's going to be like with my own eyes.

And my shorts have adorable turtles and fish on them

that make me giddy just thinking about. I can be cute and sweet, and no one's around to admonish me for not being the perfect young man I'm supposed to be. I don't have to be serious and boring anymore. As soon as I get to my room, I'm rescuing Chippy and Snap from the depths of my suitcase. I know soft toys don't need to breathe, but it's been awfully dark for them in there this whole time.

Oh! Oh! Oh! And my room—or should I say my *villa*—has its own hot tub! They all do here! There are dozens of little houses built down the hillside, and each of them is like its own VIP suite.

As it says in the resort name. Paradise.

There are golf cart-type buggies for guests to travel between the main resort and the villas, but I'm too full of energy. I just want to walk after being on the plane for so long. Besides, my case is on wheels so I can drag it most of the way and manage any steps down I come across.

I'm looking for number fifty-six, so I follow the small wooden signposts nestled in the leaves by the side of the path, finding my way. I'm so close! Once I reach the right turn-off, I practically run down the side path. All the villas are on stilts—I assume to encourage the wildlife not to wander in—so that means one must lug one's suitcase up some steps to the porch. But I do it easily with all my pumping adrenaline. Quickly getting my keycard out, I tap the door handle, and…

And nothing.

The little light stays red. But the nice lady at the desk said it would go green. I frown, checking the number. Yes, this is fifty-six. What's going on? I tap it several more times, getting increasingly upset. Now my adrenaline is fading, and I just feel exhausted. There's no way I want to trudge all the way back up to the lobby, so I start pushing on the handle even though I know that's probably not going to do any good.

"Oh, fiddlesticks!" I shout, willing myself not to cry even though my eyes are stinging. "Come on! Please!"

I just need to do this one last bit of adulting. I don't want to trip at the last hurdle! This door is all that's standing between me and the space I need to finally become my true little self, and I'm not going to let it win! I push and bang and curse and—

And suddenly, it opens.

When I see what's on the other side, I wonder if I really *have* died and gone to heaven.

CHAPTER 3
Thomas

I'M USED TO TRAVELING LONG HOURS AND WITH UNFAMILIAR hotel rooms. But every time, somehow there's still nothing quite like that first shower to wash the journey off your skin. I feel like a new man as the steaming hot water cascades down my tired muscles. My busted knee is especially appreciative after all that time sitting on the plane. Even with the extra legroom, the cabin pressure just plays havoc with it.

And this isn't some sterile motel bathroom, either. Oh no. This is an open-air rainfall shower. Well, almost. Presumably, they want to keep the creepy crawlies out. But there's a floor-to-ceiling window that looks onto a wall of tropical leaves and vines. There's a circular flagstone to stand on, but it's surrounded by big, gray pebbles that make me feel like I'm down on the beach. The walls are wooden slats. The shower-head itself is massive, making it seem like I'm under a real waterfall.

Paradise.

Or it's close, at least. What would make it truly perfect would be if I had a sweet boy getting clean by my side, preferably after some delicious lovemaking. I do my very best not to picture a certain hopeless young British man, especially since I somehow managed not to see him once on the flight or anytime between leaving the plane and getting out of the airport. He's long gone, so that's probably what allows me to imagine he's there with me without too much guilt. Maybe on his knees, blinking up at me with water droplets clinging to his gorgeous dark lashes as he sucks Daddy's cock until…

Fucking hell. I've barely been jerking off for a couple of minutes before I blow all over my hand. Well, that was most likely something else I needed after such a long flight.

Jet lag is a bitch, so I know my best bet is to stay awake now until a decent bedtime. As I towel off, I check the hotel information guide and see I've still got plenty of time to head back to the main resort restaurant for breakfast and a bucket load of coffee.

I don't have any activities planned for today other than the meet and greet this afternoon, so it's just going to be mingling by the pool and the restaurant for the next several hours. Perhaps I'll make friends with some of the other guests. It's so liberating knowing we're all here for the same kind of reason.

And I don't have a schedule to follow! It's been months—years—since I could wake up and just decide on a whim how my day is going to look. I feel like my lungs can expand fully for the first time in forever.

I'm still an athlete at heart, though. I miss running out in the wild, but that's too much pressure for my knee these days. However, the resort does have a gym, so a treadmill is an option, and something tells me it's going to have a good view as well. I can hit the weights and other equipment, too, not to mention swim lengths in the bigger pool.

After that glorious shower, I don't feel in a particular rush to build up a sweat just yet. Still, I drop my towel to the floor and open up my suitcase on the end of my bed, pondering what kind of outfit to wear. Shorts and a T-shirt seem safest with sneakers. That way I can go for a walk if I want and still be comfortable. I know modesty is important in Indonesia as well, even if we are in a private resort with a particularly liberal-minded set of clientele, so that sort of ensemble should cover all the important bits.

I like to unpack as soon as I arrive, so I start to arrange my clothes in the closet and dresser as I pull them out. The underwear appears to be crushed at the bottom, but that's okay, I'll get to it eventually. I'll just—

My door handle jiggles.

I snap my head in its direction, my heart rate speeding up. Did I imagine it? No, there it goes again. And again. Someone sounds like they're getting mad on the other side.

Jesus H Christ. Has some reporter or fan already tracked me down? Do they think I'm not here and are hoping to break in to steal a souvenir? Or—worse—do they know why I'm here and are hoping to get salacious information on me for a media scoop or blackmail? All my dreams of a secret getaway are quickly going down the drain, and anger rises in my chest.

Is one vacation away from the rest of the world really too much to ask?

Logic flies from my brain as I savagely decide to let them know I am most definitely inside this room and there will be no going through my trash today. They want to see Thomas Julio Beltran? They're going to get more than they bargained for.

I march over to the door, hearing whoever it is cursing as I reach for the handle. As naked as the day I was born and still damp from my blissful shower and jerk-off session, I yank the door open, ready to raise all hell.

"What?" I bark.

Then I freeze.

As does the person in front of me.

Arlington Hythe-Wandsworth.

My brain can't comprehend what's happening, so for a second I just stare at him as he stares back at me. Then he shakes himself and staggers back a step. "What are *you* doing in my *room?*" he squeaks, his pale skin blossoming pink.

Reality comes crashing back to me. The fact that I don't have a stitch of clothing on suddenly becomes horribly apparent.

"Your room?" I cry as I spin around, scoop up my towel, and rescue what's left of my dignity by throwing it around my waist. "Also, hello again."

I rest my hand on the doorframe and grin at him. Holy shit, my little cutie pie is *here* on this retreat! What are the chances of that? I decide not to even attempt to calculate them and instead just thank my lucky stars.

Arlington blinks several times, his mouth hanging open. "Hello again," he says faintly. "Am I dreaming?"

That does my ego the world of good. He looks just as flustered and excited to see me as I am him. Fucking hell. If he's here, then there's a chance he's exactly what I pegged him to be the moment I laid eyes on him.

A sweet boy in need of a Daddy.

My luck couldn't really be that good, could it? Well, after my torn and dislocated knee cut short my career in the blink of an eye, perhaps the universe owes me one?

"You're not dreaming," I assure him. "But I think you are lost. What room number were you looking for?"

"Fifty-six," he says immediately, patting down his pockets, presumably searching for the flimsy wallet his key came in. The card itself won't have the number on it, but the disposable casing will.

I frown. "Well, this is fifty-six. You got that right."

He finds what he was looking for…and his face instantly drops. If possible, his creamy skin gets even blotchier. "Oh…" he utters softly. "I'm not fifty-six. I'm sixty-five. I'm terribly sorry. How mortifying. Please forget this ever happened. I'll just…"

He turns to leave, but I wave my hands to make him stop, only just catching my towel in time before it falls. "I'm not sorry!" I blurt out. He turns around, and I'm probably giving him the goofiest grin, but I can't help it. "Now we both know we're staying here." I don't need to mention that implies that we also both have shared interests. Not just the kink. There's no way he's not interested in men by the way he keeps blushing.

"Yes, that *is* rather extraordinary," he says in that delightfully posh accent of his. He offers me a tiny smile that I lap up.

"I'm Thomas," I say, completely forgetting that I was going to introduce myself to everyone here as Tom. Ah, well. This kid doesn't strike me as a sports fan. He's certainly given no indication that he knows who I am. Besides, I kind of want him to know me by my actual name.

I stick out my hand. He looks at it skeptically for a second before slipping his against it for a shake. Such baby soft skin that it makes my heart flutter.

"Arlo," he says, finally looking back into my eyes. Then he smiles, like he's relieved. "I'm Arlo. It's a pleasure to meet you, Thomas."

I hold on to him for just a second longer than I probably should. Then I release him with a chuckle. Arlo, not Arlington. For all I know, he's been 'Arlo' his whole life. But I still get a little thrill, glad I know his preferred name and not just the very long one from his passport.

"Hi, Arlo," I say happily. "Hey, why don't you gimme a sec

to throw some clothes on and I'll help you find your actual villa, hmm?"

"Oh, no," he splutters. "I've already inconvenienced you tremendously. I couldn't—"

I lift my hand to stop him. "You ain't inconveniencing a thing. Please, let me do this for you."

I'm a Daddy, I'm trying to tell him. *Are you a boy? Would you enjoy being taken care of?*

He hesitates long enough that my resolve wavers. But then he lets out a little puff of air and gives me the sweetest, shy smile. "Thank you. That would be so very kind."

Score!

Doing my best not to wiggle in excitement, I give him a nod, then turn back to my case. Glancing over my shoulder, I can see he's also turned away to give me some privacy through the open door. I'm almost disappointed, but then I'm glad that this boy has good manners.

Without really caring for aesthetics, I pull on whatever my hands land on first. In less than a minute, I'm dressed in shorts and a tee like I'd planned with sneakers and socks. I even remembered briefs, which is quite impressive, since my mind was a hundred percent still on that young man hovering on my porch.

Part of me just wants to hurtle myself at him. I feel like I've been waiting my whole life for him. I know that's ridiculous. I'm just excited to maybe try proper Daddying for the first time ever. But it seems like too crazy a coincidence that our paths have crossed so many times already like they have.

Could it be Kismet?

Slow down, I tell myself sternly as I find my own key card and slip it into the back pocket of my shorts. I'm not going to fall for the first man I meet. I don't even know what he's looking for. Except his villa. Right now, I know he needs some help and reassurance, so that's what I'm going to give him.

"Okay, ready when you are," I declare as I close my door behind me. He turns and smiles shyly again, making my heart flip. Unsure what to say in that moment, I simply grab his case.

"Oh, no, you really don't have to," he starts to protest.

But I wink at him and start rolling the thing. "Nonsense," I say. *This is what Daddies do.*

I see the way he shivers at my wink, and that fuels me and my bum knee down the stairs. We fall into step along the path. I know his villa can't be too far away, but suddenly, my mind has gone blank. I almost never get to flirt with guys, certainly not when we are both free to flirt and know the other is gay and kinky. I want to ask what he's into, specifically, but that's so not the vibe.

"So, uh," I try, not really sure where I'm going with it.

"So you're American?" he says at practically the same time. "Oh, I beg your pardon. You were saying?"

I laugh and shake my head, grateful that he was at least able to think of a normal human question to ask.

"Nah, it's cool. Yeah, I'm a New Yorker, born and bred."

"But you flew from London?" he clarifies, which is fair.

"Yeah," I say, suddenly unsure. "I had some work stuff going on." I glance at him, but he's just nodding and watching his step as he walks. I'm glad he doesn't ask what I do. I'm so incredibly lucky that I'm on a second career path that I love. But my fame really isn't how I want to define myself during this trip.

"So you live in New York?" he asks.

Ah.

Suddenly, it hits me what he's asking. "Yeah," I admit.

And he lives in England.

It's not like the twinkly light in my eyes and butterflies in my stomach all vanish, but he's reminded me of a very important fact.

We live in different countries with none other than the Atlantic Ocean between us.

I already knew I needed to chill with all that Kismet stuff. I'm just hyped from being at a kink resort with the potential of a sweet boy dangling in front of my nose. But that's fine. A reality check was what I needed anyway. Actually, this changes nothing. We can still get together and have some fun, if that's something he's interested in. In fact, only having a week or so to do that with no expectations or strings attached will be perfect. No pressure. That was always the plan.

"Here we go," I declare as we reach his villa, and I bound up the stairs. Screw you, bum knee! It also pleases me that he's going to be staying barely a two-minute walk away. "Get that card out, and let's test this door."

He rolls his eyes as he retrieves it from his pocket. "I'm going to cringe about that until the day I die," he laments.

"Nah," I say playfully. "You'll forget all about it in a decade or two."

He winces, but he's still smiling as he taps the card to the sensor. When it goes green, he gasps and immediately looks at me. "It worked!"

It's like having my own special sunbeam. My heart melts a little more in my chest. "Hell yeah, it did," I assure him.

He rushes into the main living area of the villa, turning around slowly as he takes in the space before settling his gaze on the huge French doors that lead out to the back patio. "Thomas!" he cries, running over and sliding the door open. "There really is a hot tub! And look at that view!"

He's practically vibrating with joy, and it's hard to tear my eyes away to study the view he actually means. "Yeah," I agree. "It sure is something."

We look at each other for a moment before I come back to my senses and place his bag down in the middle of the room by the foot of his bed. "I'll let you get settled," I say. But then it's like I can't stop my mouth from talking even though my brain hasn't okayed the words that come out. "I was thinking. Did you wanna swap numbers? Then if you were feeling a bit unsure about doing anything by yourself to start with, you could drop me a message. Like for the meet and greet later. I'd happily be your buddy."

Buddy, yeah. That's the five-letter word I meant.

His eyes go wide. "Really? That's extremely kind of you. Are you sure it's not an imposition? I've already caused you so much trouble."

Not nearly enough, I think to myself. I manage to stop myself from grinning too much. Instead, I shrug and wink at him again.

"You'd be doing me a favor, really. I don't know nobody either."

He beams and pulls out his phone. "Well, in that case, I shall be chivalrous."

He winks back at me. I think my heart might stop altogether.

As we exchange digits, I think about how ten days is a pretty long time actually. Enough to get into some *real* trouble with the right kind of adorable boy. People have vacation flings all the time, after all. Why shouldn't I get a little slice of happiness for once?

Just because it'll all end soon doesn't mean it can't be special. And I can already tell that Arlington Hythe-Wandsworth—my little Arlo—is very special indeed.

CHAPTER 4

Arlo

I'M NOT SURE HOW LONG I SIT ON MY BED, JUST STARING OUT at my view, pondering everything that's happened to me in the past twenty-four hours.

Okay, I'm mostly thinking about Thomas, but who can blame me?

I can't get the image of his perfect, *completely naked* body out of my brain. It's stuck on a loop, and I can't even be cross about it because he is utterly delicious. Acres of light brown skin, plenty of soft black hair, and firm muscles that I simply want to lick all over.

Obviously, when I stop and think about it, I feel guilty. Once he realized I wasn't a burglar, he's been nothing but kind and gentlemanly to me. And here I am objectifying him.

But those *winks*. And more than that, he was being nice, because I'm almost certain he's a Daddy by the way he was talking, and that's exactly what I want! I've never felt like I did when he insisted on picking up my suitcase and helping me find my actual villa, even after I was so appallingly rude by almost breaking his door down.

This is what I've been searching for all these years.

And it doesn't have to end here! He gave me his phone number and said he wanted to go to the meet and greet together! That's doubly exciting because I was nervous about going all on my own. But if I get to spend any more time at all with Thomas, then that's a million times better.

He's safe as well. He might have come via Heathrow, but he assured me he lives in New York. So if anything were to happen between us, it's guaranteed to stay here, in Bali.

That makes me feel bold.

I've been hoping that coming here might give me the courage to be someone else. Or…no, that's not it. I think I'm hoping to set my true self free for once. However, I'm perfectly realistic and know it can't last. Thomas can't come home with me. I'm praying that if I allow myself this last (this *only*) hurrah, then I can return back to Wiltshire with my chin held high, ready to become the son my parents need me to be.

I think of the chaps I went to school with. Those who were rugby players and prefects and good at sums. That's who my parents always wished I was.

Just thinking about it makes my heart drop a little. I'm never going to be like that. It's simply not in my genetic makeup. But I have to *try*. I was born to be my father's heir. My family is relying on me to uphold our name and reputation. I must be grown-up and sensible.

That means dressing in boring clothes and paying better attention to politics and finances, all things I hate. But I'm not selfish, either. I'll be what Mummy and Pa want me to be. Even if that means…

Even if that means marrying a woman.

I bite my lip, really not wanting to think about this now. However, I'm so tired, it's like all my defenses are down. The thoughts tumble in regardless.

I think women are smashing. My cousin, Ginny, is the

best person I know in the whole wide world. The few friends I have are all young ladies, and I respect them tremendously.

But I've never in my life been attracted to one. Not even a tiny bit. The idea of having sex with any of the beautiful girls I'm acquainted with makes me feel sick and wrong. It's just another thing in my genetic makeup.

My parents expect an heir from me, though. So I guess I'll just have to find a nice woman who understands my predicament and we'll simply…make it work.

I hug Chippy and Snap to my chest and lie down on the bed, the cool pillow feeling so good under my head. No, there's no changing my fate. What Mummy and Pa say, goes.

But for the next ten days in this magical land of wonder so far from home, I am free.

That brings a smile to my face as my eyes drift closed. I just want to think about how nice everyone has been for a minute. I want to think about the stunning scenery and the fact that this whole villa is mine and mine alone for my entire stay. I can do what I want, *be* who I want…

Spend my time with who I want.

Does Thomas really want to be my friend? I'll be *such* a good friend if he lets me.

I'll be the most perfect baby boy if he wants.

Feeling naughty, I giggle to myself as I snuggle on the bed. Just the idea of being a little in front of anyone else is thrilling and terrifying to me. But if I picture myself trying it with Thomas, that worried, squirmy sensation in my tummy goes away. I just get butterflies in my heart instead.

Yeah, I think he's probably a good Daddy. Maybe a great one.

Would he be interested in being *my* Daddy, just for a short time?

I hope so. It's that hope that helps me let go, gentle darkness washing over me…

———

I wake to knocking on my door. "Arlo?"

Blinking groggily, I mumble something about being awake and rub my eyes. It takes me several seconds to remember where I am and what's going on.

Bali. I made it.

And that's Thomas at the door.

"Oh!" I squeak, tumbling off the bed and getting shakily to my feet. "Sorry! Coming!"

Feeling like I've got sea legs, I stumble across the room to eagerly open the door. He really came back! He wasn't just being polite! I open the door and…

Whoa.

How is he so handsome? Is that smile really just for me? He's leaning against the doorframe with his hands in his pockets, and he looks me up and down as his smile gets bigger.

"You fell asleep, didn't you?"

My hand flies to my head, where my hair is undoubtedly sticking up at a funny angle. I also clamp my mouth shut and take a step back, worried about my breath after such a long journey and all the food I ate.

"Um, maybe?" I mumble from a safer distance.

He glances into my villa, and I wince, aware it looks like a bomb went off in my suitcase as soon as I opened it. "Unpacking is going well, I see."

I grumble and throw my hands up. "I'm not sure where to put everything," I moan, aware I'm being a baby.

But…it feels nice to whine, as selfish as that probably is. But I enjoy having a teeny little tantrum about such a silly thing. Mummy would have overseen me putting every last sock away like I was a new inmate at her prison. I don't actually want all my clothes on the floor, nor do I wish to be disrespectful to housekeeping. But little boys don't always know how to unpack, do they?

As if reading my thoughts, Thomas juts his chin toward the room. "How about I come in and supervise?" he suggests.

My eyes go wide. I was enjoying my petty game, but I never actually meant to bother him any more than I already have. "Oh, no, I couldn't put you out like that," I protest.

He raises an eyebrow at me. It does funny things to my insides. "You missed breakfast, so I was concerned you might need some more help. That's why I'm here, Arlo. So, are you going to be a good boy and let me help?"

If possible, my knees get even weaker.

"I can be a good boy," I whisper, feeling like I'm in some sort of dream.

His smile is like warm sunshine. "I know you can," he says. "Come on. Let's start by putting away all your stuff. Did you bring anything special for the trip?"

I let him come inside as he's talking, and nod as I shut the door behind us to keep the cool air in. "Yes! I've got swim shorts and sunscreen and…"

It occurs to me that he doesn't mean holiday items.

"Ohhh." I skip over to the bed and pick up my soft toys. "This is Chippy, he's a seagull. Seagulls steal your chips when you're at the beach, you see. And this is my turtle, Snap. Did you know turtles have been around as long as the dinosaurs?" I look at my teddies proudly. "These are my friends, and they're going to help me look for treasure."

"Is that right?" Thomas asks as he perches on the end of the bed. "Is there a lot of treasure in Indonesia?"

I nod, hugging my teddies to my chest. "Pirates buried it here," I tell him matter-of-factly. "All beaches have treasure if you look hard enough!"

The fact that I can hear myself slipping into my little voice in front of another person should be alarming. But all I feel is pride and joy as Thomas beams at me like he's having the best conversation ever.

"You know, I think you might be onto something there, Arlo. Perhaps later today or tomorrow, I could take you down to the shore and we can have a look?"

I swallow around a lump in my throat, running my index finger and thumb against the ribbon-like label on Chippy's bottom. "You'd really want to do that, Thomas?" I ask in a small voice, not quite feeling little anymore. I'm nervous. This all feels a bit too perfect, and sadly, I don't trust it.

Thomas's expression softens. "I'd love to, Arlo," he says. "Can I be honest?" I nod eagerly. "I've never done this before with anyone."

"Gone to the beach?" I ask because apparently, my little side is still in charge of my brain. Maybe big me is too afraid to ask what I really mean, but Thomas seems to understand anyway.

He takes a breath, holding my gaze. "Been a Daddy."

My heart flips, and I can't help the small gasp that escapes my lungs. "Me, neither," I say in hushed tones, but then I shake my head. "I mean, not been a Daddy, obviously. But been with a Daddy or been Daddied by a Daddy or even really been little except for by myself, but it's different with other people, isn't it?"

I inhale then bite my lip, aware of the word vomit that I just threw up all over him. Thomas just chuckles, however, his eyes still all starry as he looks at me.

"That's perfect, then, isn't it?" he says softly. "We're both new and clumsy."

I can't help but scoff. "I'm the clumsy one, yes," I agree. "You seem to be startlingly perfect at everything. It's quite intimidating."

That gets a proper laugh from him, which fills me with warmth from my toes all the way up to my heart.

"How about this," he says, tilting his head. "Would you like to try being new and clumsy together? No pressure or anything. But maybe you'd like to hang out a bit, and we could try some Daddy/boy things."

Gosh, that sounds wonderful. But it also makes me a tiny bit nervous. He said no pressure, but I think I need more information. "Like what?"

"Well," he says as he looks around. "Why don't you be a good boy for Daddy and put away all your clothes? Daddy can help his baby boy put them in the right places. Then maybe as a reward, we can go down to the beach and look for pirate treasure?"

My heart feels like it wants to explode. On the one hand, that's a pretty simple plan. On the other hand, it sounds like the most perfect plan anyone has ever had.

"I can do that!" I say excitedly. But then a thought occurs to me, stopping me from moving. "But…you haven't met any other boys. I bet there are lots here. What if you'd rather be their holiday Daddy?"

Thomas gives me a warm look and holds out his hand. It's so much bigger than mine, but that feels perfect when I slip my palm against his and he gives me a little squeeze. "I said no pressure, remember? We're just trying this on for size. We can take it one day at a time. You might meet a better Daddy, after all."

I scrunch my nose up. That doesn't seem likely. I meant what I thought. Thomas seems too good to be true. But him saying that does make me feel less nervous. I might still get it wrong, but instead of ruining his special trip, he can try again with another boy if he wants. That makes me a bit sad but also less stressed to be perfect.

Mummy and Pa always want me to be perfect.

He squeezes my hand again. "What do you think, baby boy? Do you want to practice together?"

I nibble on my lip before nodding. "Yes," I say slowly. "But what about…do you just mean…" I huff, not sure I feel big enough to get the right words out. "We're just going to play pirates and such. No…grown-up games."

His eyes widen as he catches on to my meaning. "No, sweet boy," he assures me. "No pressure for anything like that at all. We'll take it nice and slow. This can just be Arlo and Daddy's nice relaxing playdate. When you wake up here, in your bed"— he pats it for emphasis —"you can decide each morning how you feel. Daddy only wants to help his boy to have fun."

I don't know why I'm hesitant. This is exactly what I wanted. I just didn't expect it to fall into my lap the second I arrived. Before I even got on the plane, actually! Am I reluctant because I feel like I don't deserve it?

Ah. That resonates somewhere deep inside me.

I've spent so many years hiding my sexuality and my true nature it's hard not to think of that part of myself as something dirty or wrong, even though I know it isn't. Maybe, deep inside, I believe that wrong things shouldn't be rewarded.

No! I'm not doing anything wrong. In fact, it's all rather sweet and innocent.

And it's only for ten days. Or even just one day if that's what Thomas and I decide. Like he said, no pressure. Although the thought of him moving onto another boy makes me want to cry. So perhaps I should stop getting in my own way and just try giving this a go?

"Daddy and Arlo go slow," I confirm, feeling little again now that my big grown-up thoughts have been better organized.

Thomas squeezes my hands. "As slow as little Arlo wants," he affirms. "We'll take everything one step at a time. Do you want to start by showing Daddy how nicely you can unpack all your belongings?"

My heart lifts. That's all I want! Just one task to focus on. Not a whole big picture. "Yes, Daddy!" I cry.

He beams at me, and it makes my tummy feel funny. I like making Daddy happy so much. "Good boy," he murmurs. "I think we're going to have lots of fun together."

I think he's right.

CHAPTER 5

Thomas

One of my earliest memories is getting on the ice.

I'll never forget the thrill of my shaky legs trying to support me as Uncle Leo gently slid me along, holding my hands tightly. I was torn between feeling like I was going to fall any second but also that I was on the verge of flying so fast like I couldn't even imagine.

That's how I'm feeling today as I walk hand in hand with Arlo to the resort's meet and greet event.

"Come on, Daddy! Come on!"

He tugs my hand and looks over his shoulder with sparkling eyes. My heart swoops in my chest, and I want to pinch myself for the hundredth time since I arrived.

I'm aware that we've had a frank discussion and that we're just trying out how this whole dynamic works together in a safe space. But I can't quite believe that this is Arlo's first time embracing his little side with anyone else before. Everything about him is so natural and carefree. It makes my insides contract just witnessing it. His adorable posh accent makes everything so much cuter and more amusing to me as well.

Thankfully, it didn't take long to get his case unpacked and his room sorted, as I was very conscious of the fact he hadn't eaten. Luckily, there are several restaurants that are part of the resort, and there are always a couple open at all times.

I already feel responsible for him, so I'm hoping to encourage him to have a balanced diet while we're hanging out. However, I'm getting the impression that he doesn't get the chance to let loose all that often. So the joy I get from watching him order and then devour a burger and fries over-rules any concerns I had about nutritional values for today at least.

Besides, I get to wipe ketchup from the corner of his mouth with a napkin, and oh boy, does that do stupid things to my heart.

It's a relief that we've taken sex off the table. As gorgeous as he is and as much as he entices me in all the right ways, taking baby steps is what's best for the both of us right now. Because this can only be a short-term arrangement whatever way you look at it, I think what Arlo needs most is freedom. It's like he hasn't been allowed to breathe. I can't quite explain how I know that, but I'm certain that's the case.

I can't help but feel like I'm getting the privilege of witnessing a butterfly emerging from his cocoon.

After our late lunch, we wander around the complex for a little while, getting familiar with the layout. The main pool areas really are something else, with three infinity pools on top of one another on the side of the mountain, the top two spilling into the ones below. The view across the jungle and out over the ocean is just breathtaking. I've been so lucky to travel a lot with my career, but I've never been anywhere quite like this before.

Speaking of my career, Arlo definitely has no clue who I am, and he happily accepted my answer when I told him I work for a charity that helps kids get opportunities that wouldn't otherwise have been available to them. In fact, he got this dreamy look on his face like he couldn't imagine a better job. Most people hear 'charity sector' and think terrible pay. But not Arlo, so it seems.

When I asked him how he spends his time, he shrugged and said his family had a business, but it was like I could see the joy leave his soul right in front of my eyes, which I was not going to stand for. I quickly changed the subject back to treasure, and he spent the next ten minutes excitedly telling me all about Zheng Yi Sao. She was a famous Chinese pirate who had an enormous fleet and lived to be almost seventy years old.

I was never very good at history, or anything that required sitting still and learning from books. I'm much better on my feet and with my hands getting shit done. But the way Arlo tells stories could have me captivated for hours.

It's almost a shame to head to the meet and greet, but after our discussion earlier, I know it's more important than ever for both of us to get more of a sense of the broader scene. I hate the idea of Arlo looking for another Daddy, but part of me is quietly confident that he's not actively going to be doing that.

When we arrive in the large open space usually reserved for yoga classes, I can already tell this is a good idea from what's on display. It's early afternoon, so the sun is still blazing, but the shade and ceiling fans help knock off some of the heat. Dozens of people are milling around with drinks in hand and plates of nibbles, so it feels busy but not too crowded.

I spot some more BDSM-themed equipment which makes me shiver not entirely unpleasantly. Although, I'm also relieved when Arlo isn't drawn to any of the crosses or benches the organizers have displayed.

He does, however, immediately zone in on the area with soft mats, bean bags, and a slew of kids' toys already scattered across the floor. Around the room, people are dressed casually or in leathers or skippy outfits designed for clubbing. But in this corner, I see a lot of cartoon-themed T-shirts and overalls from the people sitting on the floor.

My heart aches as I see their smiles. They don't look self-conscious in any way, and neither is my boy as he starts tugging hard on my hand.

He's not my boy. Not really. But just for today, I can pretend.

"Look, Daddy!" he says excitedly. "They have a Peppa Pig house!"

"I see," I say warmly, not really understanding what that is but not caring if it makes him happy.

I allow him to drag me over to the play area, then let him go, watching in awe as he skips into the middle of the group and introduces himself to the other kiddos who eagerly say hello back.

We're near one of the refreshment tables, so I grab myself a sparkling water, noting they have juice boxes out for when Arlo gets thirsty. Some of the food is also geared toward little bites like nuggets and carrot sticks. The idea of putting together a plate for my boy and feeding him while he sits on my lap almost makes me want to cry.

"How long have you guys been together?"

The low voice almost makes me jump. It takes me a second to recognize it as another British accent, but this guy is far from posh like Arlo. More like the East London accents I heard a lot on my trip recently.

He's reasonably built, like I am, with brown skin and kind, almond-shaped eyes. His smile is warm as he juts his chin at Arlo, who is already happily playing with some little piggy dolls on the mat with another boy.

"Oh!" I say as I run his question back through my head. "No, we just…I mean, yeah, we came together to this mixer, but we just met today. Or I guess technically we met yesterday or the day before, depending on what time zone you're looking at…"

Realizing I'm rambling, I trail off sheepishly. But the British guy gives me a sly grin. "Uh-huh," he says. "So just a holiday fling, yeah?"

I offer him a genuine one-armed shrug. "I don't know, but…"

"But you're smitten," the guy suggests.

I sigh and sip my water, suddenly wishing it was beer like he has. "Probably just caught up in the moment," I mumble down my bottleneck.

"Yeah, I can sympathize with that. I'm Andreas, by the way," he says, sticking his hand out.

"Tom," I reply, remembering my alter ego this time. We shake, and I glance back at the play mat. "Are *you* here with someone?"

His smile is one of pure adoration as he uses a finger to point at the sweet-looking blond my Arlo—I mean, just *Arlo* —is playing with. "That golden angel is my baby boy, Colby. And…" he squints as he looks around the room until his eyebrows jump up, and he indicates a tall and willowy young person in a butterfly kaftan and four-inch heels currently charming a group of half a dozen people. "There's my troublemaker, Jalen."

"You're all together?" I ask in awe.

Andreas nods, still watching his second boy fondly like he's checking he doesn't cause too much mischief while Andreas's back is turned. "We are," he confirms. "It all happened by accident. Fast, too," he adds, glancing at me with a knowing smile.

My chest feels like it's filled with butterflies like the one decorating Jalen's outfit, so I don't risk opening my mouth to ask something stupid like if love at first sight really exists. Especially because that's super ridiculous as I live in one country and Arlo lives in another.

Speaking of home locations… "So, you're all from the UK?" I eventually manage to reply.

To my surprise, Andreas shakes his head. "No, actually, we all live in Sydney. I moved from London because of work, and Jalen left California to be with Colby." He rolls his eyes and snorts. "That was when they both thought they were just best friends. They needed Daddy to come shake some sense into them both."

His laugh is warm, and I can't help but join in with him, even though I'm still piecing together his story. It sounds interesting.

He continues talking. "We saw this retreat advertised on whatever app it was, and immediately I knew it would be a good opportunity for Colby to explore his little side more with others like him. He's still so shy. We're working on that."

"Oh, Arlo's the same," I say without thinking. But I hope he wouldn't mind. He's being very open with all his age play, which I love. "I don't think he's allowed at home."

God, the thought breaks my heart. I don't want to push, but if we're going to be spending more time together, I'm desperate to know who's crushing this sweet boy down and making him feel like he can't be himself.

If he were mine, he'd be free to be Arlo twenty-four seven.

"Good job he's got his Daddy to take care of him, then," Andreas says with a wink, tapping his beer bottle against my sparkling water. Yeah, I think I'm going to need to upgrade soon. I take another swig, eager to hydrate, and switch to a brew.

"This is all new me, too," I admit. I'm not sure why I feel

like I can open up to this stranger. Probably because he's inviting me to and there's a kind of safety in knowing I'll never see him again. He also hasn't given me any indication that he recognizes me, so hopefully, I'm not being too naïve in talking to him.

Andreas nods, looking like he's thinking before speaking. "I had relationships before, but the boys were my first chance to be a real Daddy," he admits.

I slowly lift my eyebrows. "Really?"

He nods again. "So…not telling you how to live your life or anything…"Hhe laughs and winks at me. "But just because something is new and happening fast doesn't mean it's not genuine. That would be my one bit of advice, man to man."

"Daddy to Daddy," I quip quietly, and he laughs some more.

"Now you're getting it. Don't cockblock yourself."

I open my mouth to assure him that Arlo and I are only exploring age play, not anything sexual, but I realize it doesn't matter. In fact, if this were just sex, it wouldn't be an issue in the first place.

He means that we—specifically *I*—shouldn't be afraid of going all in on this relationship, even if it's just for our vacation. It's what we both want. We're adults, and we had a clear conversation about needs and boundaries.

The only thing that's going to spoil this experience is if I overthink it.

For the next several days, Arlo is mine if that's what he wants. I know I have no interest in looking for a different boy, not when the perfect one already fell into my lap. But judging by the way he keeps looking over at me to check I'm watching him as he plays with his new friends, I can't help but feel optimistic that he doesn't seem particularly interested in continuing his hunt for a vacation Daddy either.

Finishing off my water, I pick up a beer from the free bar,

and hold it out. With a warm chuckle, Andreas meets my eyes and clinks the bottles together.

"Cheers," he says in his thick accent, giving me a sparkling grin. I feel like he's my fairy godfather, giving Arlo and me his blessing.

So I vow to let myself just enjoy what comes and to simply wait and see what happens.

A lot can go down in ten days, after all.

CHAPTER 6

Arlo

I THINK THIS MIGHT BE THE BEST DAY EVER.

Okay…not ever in the history of the world for anyone ever. But…it might be my best day ever.

Whenever I look up, Thomas is there, watching over me and making me feel so special and important. I played on the floor with the other littles until I started yawning too much. I didn't want to stop, but then Thomas was already there with some apple juice for me as well as a plate of yummy food that he picked out for me.

He gets us to sit down at a table and makes sure I eat enough so I feel better again. He tells me all about how he's traveled for work and that jet lag can be really rubbish so one has to look after oneself.

Except *he's* looking after me, which is so much better.

The meet and greet officially finishes late in the afternoon, and it seems a lot of people are heading to the bar to keep socializing. I'm conflicted as I'm having fun, and I like making new friends, but right now, I'm relishing the chance to be freely little. It seems too soon to stop.

"Hey, baby boy," Thomas says, breaking me from my reverie. "Are you okay?"

We're sitting at one of the tables in the yoga area, which is a sort of open-walled marquee. The staff are starting to clear everything away, including the toys from the playmat. I bite my lap, almost panicking that everything is evaporating too quickly.

"Arlo?"

"Yes, Daddy?" I say without thinking, snapping my attention back to him. A slow, warm smile spreads across his face. He licks his lips before speaking, his eyes never leaving mine.

"Would you like to go play on the beach?"

For a second, I just stare at him. Eventually, I realize that he's asking if I'd like to continue being little. But this time, it'll be just with him.

"Oh, yes, please!" I screech, clapping my hands.

Thomas laughs kindly at me as a couple of the staff look over. They might think I'm strange, but in that moment, it doesn't seem to matter to me like it usually would. At home, I'm constantly trying to fit into places where I don't belong. Right now, I feel like I'm exactly where I'm supposed to be.

"Awesome," Thomas says.

I love his strong New Yorker accent. He sounds like he should be on the television or something. Maybe that's not just the way he speaks. He's got a confidence about him that makes me feel like he's often in front of people. I guess running those charity programs means he's used to dealing with rowdy children and such.

"May we please go now?" I ask eagerly. I know that in Bali, the sun sets around six or seven-ish. It would be so cool to see that.

Thomas chuckles. "Let's go change into swim shorts first just in case we want to go in the water. And Daddy might have a surprise for you, too."

I blink at him. "A surprise?" I ask weakly. "But…we only just met?"

He gently places his hand over mine. I raise my eyebrows. Gosh, that feels nice. When I smile at him, he seems to understand that I like it, and relaxes. "I hoped I might meet a special boy, so I packed some fun presents that I hoped to share with him."

"And him is me?" I ask.

He laughs again. "That's right, baby boy."

I squirm in my seat. "Thank you, Daddy," I whisper, not quite believing how lucky I am.

Just as I'm about to jump up from my seat, I feel something tickle against my bare leg. I look down to see a huge, fluffy orange cat twirling around my feet.

"Oh!" I squeak, reaching my hand down to offer them my fingers to sniff. "Aren't you gorgeous!"

Okay, so he might be a bit matted in places, but it's still true. He's a beauty, and once he's sniffed my fingers, he starts rubbing his face against my hand.

"Be careful, hon," Thomas says, sounding concerned.

"Aww," I coo down at my new friend. "He's a sweetheart."

A snort nearby makes me look up. A young female employee is tidying away some of the food from the buffet. Her name badge reads 'Kirana,' and she grins at me. "Kucing mean to everybody," she says, pronouncing it like 'ku-*ching.*' "You special, he like you."

"Does he?" I cry, ridiculously pleased. I can feel Kucing purring against my skin. Have I really been chosen by both a Daddy *and* a cat? Growing up, Mummy and Pa never let me have pets. They said they were messy and undignified. But I always wanted a cat or a dog or even a rabbit or a budgie.

Anything that might let me love it and be my unconditional friend.

Kirana abandons her stack of plates and comes over to

smile at us, then puts her hands on her hips as she looks down at the cat. "Kucing my friend but I…" She frowns, thinking about the word, then mimics a sneeze.

"Oh, you're allergic?" I guess.

She snaps her fingers and nods at me. "Yes. But I feed him, and he no bite me." She cackles, like she admires that he's so fierce and can be won over with a good dinner. She spins around to get a plate off the table with some slices of meat on it. "You and your boyfriend feed Kucing?"

I blush and glance at Thomas. "Oh, um…" I say, feeling flustered.

But Thomas smiles at her as he reaches out to take the proffered plate. "We'd love to. Thank you."

Biting my lip and still blushing horribly, I can't help but smile at Thomas. Obviously he's *not* my boyfriend. But I like that he didn't bother to correct the nice waitress. She gives us two thumbs up, then gathers up the pile of crockery she put down when she came over to us, and bustles back toward the kitchen.

I pick up a slice of white meat, roll it up, then hold it out for Kucing to inspect. He sniffs it but then just looks at it.

"Here," Thomas says, beckoning with his fingers for me to give him the chicken or whatever it is. He gets a little side plate and quickly rips up the meat along with another slice. "There. Try that now."

Kucing is still watching me as I take the plate and put it on the floor by my feet. Again, he steps closer and sniffs it. But this time his little pink tongue flicks out and he takes a bite. Within seconds, he's gobbling up the lot.

Not wishing to disturb him in case it scares him off, I don't make a sound. But I clutch my hands into fists and beam at Thomas, who smiles back at me with a nod.

I know it's silly, but it feels like we did that together. We worked as a team. He didn't take over or dismiss me. I feel respected.

Plus, the joy of winning over a reportedly grumpy cat gives me a deep sense of satisfaction.

We quietly watch Kucing until he's licked the plate clean, then he scampers off to sit by one of the wooden beams that's keeping the roof up. He proceeds to start licking his paw and rubbing his face, having a post-dinner wash.

Happy that I've done a good deed, I hop off my chair and smile at Thomas. "Beach now, Daddy?" I ask.

He chuckles at me and stands up himself. "Swim trunks, sunscreen, *then* beach," he says in a warm but no-nonsense tone.

I open my mouth to protest that it's creeping toward the end of the afternoon and that we probably don't need extra suntan lotion. But then I think about Thomas's hands rubbing slippery cream all over my back.

"Okay, Daddy!" I reply eagerly. "Race you back home!"

I'm aware that it's not really 'home,' but I know Thomas gets what I mean. However, as soon as I break into a run, Thomas cries out after me.

"Whoa there, slugger!"

I turn and see he's raised his hands and is looking sheepish as he walks toward me. I raise my eyebrows and trot back to meet him.

"I'm sorry, Daddy," I say in a small voice, upset I've done something wrong. I was just so excited!

But he shakes his head and reaches to take my hand. My heart leaps as I let him, loving how he rubs the backs of my knuckles.

"Daddy's got a bum knee, sweetheart." He looks down at his right leg apologetically. "I have to be careful when I run, and warm up properly and all that other boring grown-up stuff."

Immediately, my heart lifts in relief. I didn't do anything wrong! I just didn't know, but now I do. But then I feel bad again. I shouldn't be happy. Thomas has an injury.

Perhaps there's something I can do to help? My heart lifts once more.

"Oh, Daddy has a poorly knee! Arlo kiss it better!"

Not really sure what I'm doing, I drop his hand which makes him stop walking, then I crouch down and press my lips noisily to his hairy knee. His skin is warm and tastes salty from sweat and previously applied sunscreen. I giggle at the silliness of what I've just done, but then I look up at Thomas through my lashes.

Oh.

He's looking down at me with wide eyes, and takes a deep breath as our gazes meet. It occurs to me in that moment what crouching in front of him like this also puts me in front of.

I know I want to take things slow. We both do. I'm sure somewhere in the back of my mind I can even remember why. But in that moment, all I can think is how much I'd love to free my Daddy's cock and swallow it all the way down so he makes the most delicious noises. After the way he's taken care of me, I want to make him feel so, so good.

But then he clears his throat, grins, and offers me his hand so I can stand back up again.

"It's a miracle!" he exclaims. "I'm cured!" He gives his leg a jiggle that makes me laugh, and suddenly, all those complicated, sexy, adult feelings drift away.

I've done a lot of that before, and it never really ends up with the other guy acting the way I wanted. Those boys at school always just sort of took me for granted and never told me I was good or that they liked what I did the way I hoped. Well, except for Chris. He was always nice and looked out for me. Until he went away to university, at least.

Anyway, enough thinking about all that nonsense. What I *haven't* done a lot before is get to run around like a silly person, not even when I was tiny. Neither of my parents was afraid to issue a swift slap if I acted too childishly out in public, so I learned at a very young age to mind my manners.

It took me until I was grown to realize that a little frivolity done respectfully doesn't hurt a soul.

As Thomas walks normally, I zoom around him with my arms outstretched. "Look, Daddy! I'm an albatross following your pirate ship!"

"Oh, dang it!" he cries in mock distress. "Ain't albatrosses bad luck?"

I stop flying and wrinkle my nose at him. "Only if you shoot them down, Daddy," I say.

He raises his eyebrows. "I did not know that. Clever boy."

When he ruffles my hair, I hum in delight and start flying around again, protecting our ship until we make it back to our rooms.

Thomas goes right, and I go left. I only pout for a second that we part ways, because I realize that if we each go separately, we'll be back quicker than if we went to one villa then another. That means we'll get to the beach sooner.

Excited, I race up to my door and let myself inside, stripping off my clothes before the door has even closed fully.

As I hurriedly drag my trunks up my legs, I look back at the trail of clothes I left in my wake. My little wants to leave them there, seeing as Mummy isn't here to scold me about them. But then I think of Thomas and how he kindly helped me unpack earlier. Everything was so nicely in its place until I came back in.

The urge to make Thomas proud, even if he isn't here, is what draws me back over the room to pick everything up. I hang the slightly damp T-shirt and shorts over the sides of the wicker armchair to dry off, then put the underwear in the tote bag I specifically packed for that purpose. I know the resort has a laundry room somewhere. Not that I know where it is or how I would use anything.

That's a problem for another day. Right now, I'm proud that my room still looks nice, and I've got my octopus-patterned shorts on, ready for the beach. I shove my feet back into my flip-flops, grab my key card, and go.

Of course Thomas is the one who remembers the sunscreen. And hats for us both. And a spare T-shirt for me in case I get cold. And it turns out that his surprise is a brand-new bucket and spade set that also has molds in the shapes of starfish and seahorses and the like.

As we go down to the water to play in the sand and watch the sun set, I think I might have been right earlier.

This really has been the best day ever.

I wonder what tomorrow will be like.

CHAPTER 7
Thomas

THIS BOY IS GOING TO BE THE DEATH OF ME.

In so many ways, he's everything I want. He's so free with his age regression. I just love watching him visibly let go before my eyes. We spend a couple of hours on the beach playing around and splashing in the waves, not a care in the world. It's everything I've dreamed of.

Except I can't shake the knowledge that the clock is ticking even though we only just got here. That this is the reason I'm keeping my distance from him physically when all I want to do is pull him into my lap and smother kisses all over his face. He said he doesn't want a sexual relationship, and when we're going to have to say good-bye in a little over a week, it makes sense to keep that distance.

But it doesn't make sense at all.

His lithe, pale body is so perfect to me. I just want to lick him all over. When he was down on his knees for me earlier, his wet lips parted as he looked up at me with those beautiful hazel eyes, I was so close to totally losing it.

How can something so perfect also be driving me completely nuts after just one day? One lousy day?

So yeah, R.I.P. me. Or at least my poor, neglected dick. He doesn't agree with the upstairs brain that being a gentleman is absolutely the right thing to do.

Still, the second I flop onto the bed and close my eyes, it doesn't stop me from gloriously jerking off to thoughts of that sweet boy and his sunshine smile.

I'm only human. So sue me.

Once I spurt all over my hand and chest, I at least have the presence of mind to clean up before I pass out. Thanks to my captivating and energetic companion, I managed not to get drowsy all day despite my jet lag. But after that orgasm, I'm a goner the second my head hits the cool pillow again.

Or so I thought.

The chime of my message alert makes me groan. My family, friends, and colleagues all know I'm on a damn vacation. I told them it was okay to bother me while I was in London because that was a work trip. But this is the first *me* time I've really taken in years. Whoever is bugging me is going to get an earful over text.

However, as soon as I see the name on my screen, I realize it's none of those people that have written to me. I'm wide awake again, my blood pumping.

Ironic, considering the nature of the text.

ARLO: Daddy, I can't sleep

He's added several ridiculous but adorable emojis afterward. I grin and shake my head. What a naughty boy I have on my hands, clearly after attention when he should be resetting his sleep pattern.

THOMAS: Lol. Close your eyes and count sheep

I add a winky, kissy emoji of my own, something I'd never do in 'real life.' It's crazy, but I feel like a damn teenager with a crush, willing the dots to appear to tell me he's writing back.

They do. I let out a hiss of relief.

ARLO: Sheep are boring, Daddy

More emojis that tell me how funny he thinks he is. I laugh in the quiet of my villa, but then I frown and pretend to be stern as I type.

THOMAS: That's the point, baby boy. They're supposed to lull you to sleep

'Lull'? Who even am I right now? I'm still grinning and shaking my head, though, as I wait for his response.

ARLO: Can I count flying fish instead?

So cute.

THOMAS: Of course, sweetheart. Now get some rest. We're going to have more fun tomorrow

He sends me a single heart, which beats on my screen.

ARLO: Okay, Daddy. Night night. Sweet dreams.

THOMAS: Right back atcha, baby boy

I'm slightly disappointed when, after a minute, it seems obvious that more messages aren't coming. But then I'm proud. My boy listened to his Daddy and did what he was told.

Good boy.

I plug in my cell to charge, and this time I don't fight the sleep that immediately comes to me, a smile still on my lips.

———

Of course I wasn't going to escape jet lag that easily. I find myself wide awake at five the next morning, but considering that I usually drag my ass out of bed at six or seven-ish anyway to do physical therapy and work out, it's not too terrible.

In fact, after ten minutes of staring at the ceiling fan and realizing I'm not going to get back to sleep anytime soon, I figure why not stick to my usual routine anyhow? It's clear that if I'm going to be hanging with Arlo, he's going to be keeping me on my toes. So it would be good for my knee if I keep up my therapy. I drop him a message to let him know where I am and what I'm doing as I won't check my phone once I get going, then head out.

As I suspected, the treadmills face windows that display the spectacular vista, and that helps my mind to wander, easing some of my concerns. So not only am I helping keep my damaged muscles and ligaments strong, but this also helps me clear my head.

I spent half of yesterday preoccupied with the idea that the time limit Arlo and I face will spoil our time together, when it's the opposite that's true. It's going to be freeing for both of us.

After my accident, I got so bitter and angry that Mama had enough in the end and threatened to hit me with a wooden spoon if I didn't go talk to someone professionally. The thought of spilling my guts to a stranger filled me with dread, and I barely said three words that first session.

But I went back the next week.

After a couple of months, I could see how much seeing a shrink was helping me understand where all my anger was coming from. I felt out of control thanks to an injury that only took a matter of seconds to basically ruin my life. Except it *didn't.* I found the strength to move on to the next awesome chapter of my life.

More importantly, it helped me to accept that there is so much in this world that's completely out of my control, no matter how hard I try to manage everything. Like this vacation. I have to accept that even though my feelings for Arlo have come on hard and fast, there's only so far they can go.

There's a calmness to that acceptance.

By the time I shower and head back from the gym to my villa, I'm feeling much more confident about being the Daddy Arlo needs me to be. I'm a safe space for him to finally live out his age-play desires. While I get the impression that he's not exactly inexperienced when it comes to other desires, for whatever reason he doesn't want that right now.

So I will give him what he wants and not worry about the rest.

Part of what I can control and what I've enjoyed so far is being the one to make plans or at least suggest them. Arlo seems to get a kick out of being cared for that way, too.

Therefore, when I pass by reception and see a poster advertising a bus that goes every hour to a nearby market, I immediately text Arlo to see if he'd like to do that today. I'm not sure about him, but personally when I visit a place, I like to actually see the local culture instead of just lying by the pool the entire time.

Judging by Arlo's enthusiastic response, he feels the same way.

I chuckle at the dozen or so emojis that accompany his reply before telling him I'll meet him outside his villa once I've gone back to mine. I'm dressed appropriately for a shopping excursion, but I need to dump my gym bag and grab my wallet as well as some cash from my safe. According to the internet, credit cards aren't always accepted at market stalls. Also, haggling is encouraged, which I'm looking forward to. I've always enjoyed a challenge.

As it turns out, I'm not the only one waiting for Arlo on his porch. A familiar scruffy orange cat is sitting on the deck, his tail swishing back and forth as he eyes me up warily.

"Hey, there," I say, equally suspicious of him as he is of me. Arlo might be won over, but I can agree with Kirana from the resort that Mr. Kitty here looks like he'll play dirty as soon as your back is turned.

Kucing glares at me for a few more seconds, then turns in a circle before settling down on the wooden boards. Grateful that I haven't been deemed a threat, I walk the final few steps and knock on Arlo's door.

"Coming!" he shrieks as I hear something thud to the floor, followed by some muttering. I laugh again.

"No rush, baby boy," I assure him truthfully. If we miss this bus, we'll just take the next one. We're on vacation, after all. There's no schedule aside from the one we make for ourselves.

Still, Arlo opens the door suddenly, breathless but grinning as soon as he sees me. "Daddy!" he squeaks. My heart contracts and I don't think I'll ever get tired of being called that. "I'm ready to go!"

I hum, unconvinced. "Where's your hat?"

"Oh."

I snort as he spins around and grabs a baseball cap from off his dresser. "And have you put sunscreen on?"

"Uhh…"

Laughing and shaking my head, I wrap my fingers around his wrist and tug him out onto the porch, sitting down on one of the chairs by the table. "It's okay. Daddy's gotcha." I wink as I pull out a bottle of lotion from my backpack and start applying it to his exposed arms and legs.

Arlo grins sheepishly at me, but then he spots his other guest. "Oh! Jolly's still here!"

"Jolly?" I repeat. "I thought his name was Kucing?"

Arlo giggles and squirms as I smear lotion over his pale face. "When you said you were at the gym, I went to get some breakfast and ran into him again. I asked one of the other staff members, and he told me that 'kucing' just means 'cat.' He said Kirana didn't want to name him properly so she wouldn't get too attached. So I decided to call him Jolly instead."

It's on the tip of my tongue to fret that Arlo shouldn't get attached either, but I don't want to mention the elephant in the room and spoil our mood. So I say "Jolly?" instead. "Because he's so cheerful?"

Arlo laughs again, skipping away now that I'm done protecting him from the sun. "No, the opposite. Jolly as in Jolly Roger—because he's so fierce he scares people away."

It's my turn to laugh at the irony. "Good pick," I say, nodding in appreciation. "That's clever."

"I fed him again," Arlo informs me as he lets the cat rub his head against his fingers. "And the waiter said there's a place that sells pet stuff at the market, so I was going to try and buy a brush so I could have a go at untangling his fur."

Good luck with that, I think, but I don't say anything to dampen Arlo's enthusiasm. In fact, I think it's extremely admirable that he wants to help the creature out. I doubt Jolly will appreciate it, but if Arlo can sort any of those mats out, I'm sure his little furry friend will feel better for it.

Jolly follows us all the way to the front of the resort, much to the amusement of several staff members. But then he sits on the steps to watch us wait for the bus, staying there until we board. Arlo waves to him through the window until he disappears from view.

I almost worry about how sad he's going to be when he has to leave the cat behind, but then I remind myself to live in the moment and let go of the things I can't control.

Today is about exploring a new place with my excitable boy.

The market is buzzing despite it being a weekday. I suppose that doesn't matter when it's a tourist area. I'm immediately taken by all the art stalls selling wooden and metal crafts as well as paintings, jewelry, and knick-knacks. There are also plenty of places offering souvenirs, clothes, beach paraphernalia, and the like.

There's a ton of different foods being offered, both sweet and savory. I get us two bowls of fried rice with veggies and chicken, as well as a fried egg on top as apparently that's a traditional go-to. Arlo doesn't mind a second breakfast and I certainly need a first after my work-out. It's delicious, and I envision slowly eating our way around the market as we browse all the wares as a very pleasant way to spend the day.

I'm so wrapped up in my daydream that I'm completely blindsided when a group of surfer-looking dudes shove their way between Arlo and me, roughhousing and shouting at each other in Australian accents.

"Hey, watch it!" I holler as I steady Arlo back on his feet. They almost spun him all the way around, for god's sake. Luckily, we've finished our food by this point and disposed of the cardboard bowls so my hands are free to check over my boy.

"Up yours, grandpa!" one of them crows as his buddies cackle. They're racing down the street, bouncing off people and objects like they're a pack of wild dogs.

I tut and shake my head before turning my attention back to Arlo. "Are you okay?" I ask.

He laughs, but he sounds a bit shaken at getting pushed like that. His face is flushed as well. "Yeah, I'm fine. I…"

He's patting the pockets in his shorts when he freezes, all color draining from his face. "Arlo?" I prompt.

"My wallet," he whispers in horror, his eyes darting to the retreating gaggle of boys. "It's gone."

I don't think.

I just start running.

CHAPTER 8

Arlo

I don't realize what's happening before it's too late. I'm so horrified when the knowledge that I've been pickpocketed hits me that I don't understand what Thomas is doing.

Until he's bolting after the thieves.

"No!" I cry, immediately chasing after him.

It's not that I don't want my property back. But yesterday he didn't even want to play-race me back to our villas. Now he's sprinting through this market like he's James Bond and they've just stolen the nuclear codes.

It's incredibly admirable, and there's a part of me that swells with pride that he would do that for me.

But that all vanishes as soon as he stumbles to a halt, clutching his knee. Even from a dozen feet away, I can see the grimace on his face.

"Sorry! I'm so sorry!" I say as I rush up to him, already worried that he's going to be mad at me. He shakes his head and frowns at me.

"Aw, kid, *I'm* sorry. Those bastards got your wallet, and I couldn't catch them. Fuck!" He looks so mad, and my heart stutters in my chest.

"Your knee," I whimper miserably.

But he waves his hand and straightens up. "Nothing a bit of ice won't fix, I'm sure," he says dismissively, although I'm not convinced. "I hope you didn't have much money on you."

"To buy ice?" I say. Then I realize how stupid that is. If we have to buy ice, Thomas still has his wallet and…

Oh…

Oh *no*.

"They took my wallet," I say as the gravity of the situation dawns on me. My hand is already shaking as I clamp it over my mouth, tears springing into my eyes. I am so *fucked!*

"Hey, hey," Thomas says urgently. It's like he forgets about his pain in a second as he grabs my shoulders and looks at me with concern. "Sweetheart, it's fine."

I shake my head, but I can't make the words come out. Thomas glances around, spying a little coffee place with a free table outside, so he steers us to sit down. It's a good plan for both of us, as he obviously needs to take the weight off his knee, and I feel like I'm about to pass out. I think he maybe signals to someone to order drinks, but I'm too busy spiraling to really be sure.

"Arlo," Thomas says firmly. "Arlo, please look at me." When I do, he smiles so brightly at me that for a second I think he's right. Things really will be okay. "There we go. Good boy. Now, I'm so sorry that just happened to you, but believe me when I say it's just money. The resort is all inclusive anyway, and if you want to buy anything more at the market, Daddy will take care of it."

I blink and hiccup, guilt and awe warring within me. I love that he wants to do that, but I've only known him a day. I couldn't possibly impose upon him like that. We'd only just finished our food and haven't even started shopping yet. I wanted to get some things for Jolly but also some silly trinkets for *me*. Who knows if I'll ever get the chance to take a holiday like this again, and I wanted some souvenirs to remember it by.

But that's really not the problem at hand.

I gulp down air and try to form some words. Thomas is still shaking his head. "Baby, please believe me when I say that it's not a problem at *all*. I've got plenty of money. I really want to make this okay, and there's nothing here I wouldn't buy if it would make you smile again."

Biting my lip, I try to offer him a smile. "That's so sweet," I manage to whisper. "Thank you. But…"

He brushes his thumb against my cheeks, wiping the tears away. It's so gentle and intimate it takes my breath. For a second, I just stare at him. He's the one in pain, yet he's looking at me like his only concern in the whole world is my wellbeing.

I'm so *stupid*. Why didn't I think like a proper adult? It's all well and good wanting to be a little and shirk my responsibilities, but the fact is that I'm a grown-up. Mummy and Pa are right. It's my duty to inherit the company and continue the family name with honor, but the truth is that I'm a useless baby who can't be trusted with anything and—

"Arlo!" Thomas snaps firmly. I wonder if it's not the first time he said my name just then. But if he wanted my attention, he's got it. I blink and take a deep breath. He'd had his hands on either side of my face, but as a waitress approaches with a tray, I pull back both to give her room and to put a bit of distance between Thomas and myself.

It was feeling a tad too intimate for a public space.

I clear my throat and thank the waitress as she places two coffees in front of us. There doesn't look to be any milk, but there is sugar which I think is what I need right now. Thomas needs something else as well, though.

"Um, excuse me," I say as the waitress goes to leave. "Do you have any ice?"

She raises her eyebrows and looks between me and my drink. "You want iced coffee instead?" she says amicably.

I wave my hands. "Oh, no. I'm sorry. My friend hurt his leg." I point to Thomas's knee.

"Oh!" the waitress says with an understanding smile. "Of course. One minute, please."

I think it's amazing how everyone seems to be able to speak at least a little English here, if not fluently. I did French and Latin at school, and I was terrible at both no matter how hard I tried.

After the waitress bustles back inside the little café, I look back to see Thomas smiling at me, but there's something else on his face as well that I can't quite read. "Sorry, did I over-step?" I ask.

He shakes his head and sighs, but I think it's a happy noise. "You're just a very special boy, Arlo. I should be taking care of you, not the other way around."

And just like that, all my panic and shame come rushing back. "You've only known me a couple of days," I insist, feeling my cheeks flushing and my eyes stinging with tears. "I don't want to be your problem."

But the truth is that I don't know what the *hell* I'm going to do. This is a disaster. Am I going to have to call home and ask for help?

The mere thought makes me inhale sharply, and my hands start shaking again. If I have to admit where I am and what I was doing…I don't think my parents will ever let me live down the disgrace. Preemptive humiliation washes over me.

The only thing that snaps me out of it is Thomas gripping my hand and squeezing it tight. I blink and realize that the waitress must have already returned and left again because in his other hand is a cloth bundled against his knee, and I assume it's got a plastic bag of ice wrapped up inside of it.

"Arlo, you are not a problem," Thomas tells me firmly. "When I said I wanted to be a Daddy on this getaway, I meant it. And yeah, that means nice things like packing you snacks and making sure you're covered in enough sunscreen. But honestly? If I get to help you with a *real* emergency, that's like a dream to me. Not that I want you to be in trouble," he adds with raised eyebrows to clarify. "But this is what I've longed for. I need to be needed. So you are not a burden or a problem, okay?"

Taking a shaky breath, I nod. But he doesn't understand the extent of the situation, and he won't until I tell him.

Bloody hell, how could I have been so irresponsible?

"Thomas," I say heavily. "I…I haven't traveled much. I think I'm a bit naïve. I thought…I really wasn't sure about trusting the hotel safe. I thought it would be better to keep everything on me. But I didn't even feel that boy lift the wallet from my pocket." I scowl bitterly and try to blink away any more tears.

Thomas doesn't seem perturbed as he reaches up and cups the side of my face again. "So you had all your money on you," he guesses.

I nod miserably. "Those boys are going to be so happy when they realize they've hit the jackpot."

"Fuck them," Thomas growls with such force it shocks me out of my fugue for a moment. "I told you—money isn't a problem for me. I'm so sorry you were violated like that, but you really don't have to give it a second thought."

"I had almost a thousand pounds in Rupiah on me," I admit feebly. How could I have been *so* foolish?

But when I peek back at Thomas, his expression hasn't shifted. I don't understand.

"Don't you work for a charity?" I ask, trying to make sense of his reaction. That's a lot of money! Not for Mummy and Pa, obviously. But I worked hard to save all that up, and now it's just *gone.*

Unfortunately, he laughs. It's not unkind in the slightest, but it doesn't do anything to explain what's going on. "I had a different job before that, sweetheart," he says, stroking my cheek. It sends butterflies through my chest. "I don't want to be a dick about it, but I really can take care of you. Hell, if I thought you'd let me, I'd withdraw that right outta an ATM for you this second."

"No, no!" I splutter. I definitely don't want that. But… okay. So perhaps he's telling the truth, and I really don't have to fret so much about accepting his extremely kind offer to help me out with the money situation.

He takes his hand off my face to hold it up in a gesture of defeat, chuckling. "I know, I know. But would you at least consider allowing me to be your sugar Daddy, just for today? We came here to go shopping, after all."

He winks, and I wish it were that simple. In fact, that could have been quite fun if it hadn't started in disaster. But we can't buy what I need here.

"I…I…" My throat has clamped up again as I struggle to maintain control over my emotions. I need to be strong. I need to be responsible. But all I want to do is crumple to the ground and wail.

"Arlo," Thomas says with such compassion it makes my heart shudder and my lower lip wobble. "Talk to me."

"That wasn't actually my wallet," I blurt out. "I was just using it as one."

Thomas frowns. "Then what was it, sweetheart?"

I take a shaky breath and make myself look into his brown eyes despite the shame that's engulfing me. "It was my passport holder," I utter, feeling like I'm unraveling. "They didn't just get my money. They got my room key card and my passport, too. I'm stranded here. I can't get back to England."

With that, I burst into tears again.

CHAPTER 9
Thomas

I don't care who's around. I know in Indonesia, it's important not to show too much PDA. But this is an emergency. My boy is distraught.

"Hey, hey," I coo, trying to soothe him as I pull him into my lap. He sits across my thighs, so it's not indecent. He curls into a ball against my chest. "It's okay, Arlo, I promise."

I knew it was more than about the money, although I can easily see why he'd be so upset at losing everything. Getting robbed like that is a violation, too. He has plenty to be rattled about.

But his passport?

Jeez.

It's hard not to get mad at myself. That won't help anyone now, but before my knee got blown out, I know I could have chased those douchebags down without breaking a sweat and saved the day. It's hard not to feel like I've been betrayed by the body I spent my whole life relying on and taking for granted.

Except…actually, I have no idea which little shithead was the one to pickpocket my boy. I would only have been able to catch one of them if I'd been fit enough to keep running, and as there had been half a dozen of them, the chances are good I wouldn't have grabbed the right kid anyway.

Fuck.

So in a way…my injury is irrelevant. Once I take a breath and squeeze Arlo against me, I see that clearly. What's done is done. All I can do now is whatever's in my power to fix this.

And when I take a minute to reason it through, it's easy to see that Arlo clearly thinks he's way more fucked than he actually is.

"Baby boy," I say as I lean back to look into his eyes. They're still pretty despite all the tears. "You're not stranded here."

"I'm not? But…?"

I hate to let him go, but I can feel people looking and I don't want us to get in trouble for being inconsiderate on top of everything else. I can handle a slap on the wrist, especially as we are taking liberties. But Arlo doesn't need anything else to upset him right now.

So I encourage him to slip back into his seat. Then I go the extra mile and put three teaspoons of sugar in his coffee, stir it, and hand it to him. "Have a sip," I encourage him. "It'll fortify you."

He sniffs it. "I usually drink tea," he admits.

I chuckle. "I know, but I think you need a little kick-start. I've made it sweet, and it's kind of fruity. Can you try it for me?"

I was hoping to distract him from spiraling, and I think I've succeeded. He cradles the cup and takes a small sip, his eyebrows raising. "Oh," he says.

"Okay?" I ask. I have to admit I quite like the coffee here as a change from the usual western style.

"Yeah, different," he admits, taking another little sip.

Excellent. I rub his back and watch as he stops shivering. Taking a gulp of my own cup, I can feel him calming down a fraction as the caffeine helps him straighten out his thoughts.

"Right," I say, taking charge of the situation. There might be a lot about this relationship that's outside of my control, but this I can handle. "People lose their passports all the time abroad."

Arlo's eyes go wide. "Really?"

I bite back a laugh, not wanting him to think I'm mocking him. But his innocence is so adorable I can't stop my heart from melting a little.

"Of course," I assure him. "People get robbed like you do, or they just lose them. I had a buddy who left his in the seat pouch on the plane."

I roll my eyes at that memory. The two of us had ended up running all through the airport after the crew had rightfully sent the damn thing to lost property. But it had meant we'd missed our connecting flight, and Coach had almost cut us from the game after missing practice.

But recalling that makes me more determined to get it through Arlo's head that he's not a burden at all. "This was *not* your fault, okay?"

He shakes his head. "I shouldn't have taken it out of the hotel room. It's just Mummy always says..." He trails off, biting his lip. "She never trusts staff coming into the room. It's unfair. Why I would think a locked safe in a five-star resort with staff who've been nothing short of kind and welcoming would be risky is just..." He pulls another face. "I don't want to be like that."

"You're not," I assure him. "You're still learning. You'll think differently next time."

Arlo has a good soul and a trusting nature. That's very easy to see. But the way he talks about his folks makes me think that he hasn't come from the best type of people. My abuela cleaned offices her whole working life, making sure my mom and her siblings never wanted for nothing. And there was always some asshole who'd show up every now and again accusing her of stealing.

My boy isn't like that, though. He's just been lacking in good role models, I'm damned sure.

Lucky for him, he's got a hothead Daddy now, even if it's just for a week.

"Okay, here's what we're going to do," I say with a bright smile. "We're going to go to the embassy right now and sort this all out."

He frowns. "The…embassy?" he says uncertainly. "But isn't that where politicians go?"

I shake my head. "Yes, but they're just as much for the people, too. Think of it as a little pocket of home, ready and waiting to help its citizens out of a jam day or night."

He frowns and chews his lip. "But I don't know where it is or how to get there," he says in a rush. "Does one need an appointment? What if—?"

"Shhh, baby boy," I say as I rub his knee. The skin-to-skin contact sends shivers down my spine, but this isn't the time or place, so I try to ignore it. Especially when the intimate touch seems to shock him out of worrying. "This is what Daddies are for. I've got it all covered."

He looks at me incredulously. "Really?" Then he shakes his head. "Blimey, of course you do. You run your own charity. You must think—"

Before he can say something unkind about himself, I hold up my finger. To my delight, he stops speaking right away. "I think that you are a sweet, trusting boy who got himself screwed by accident. I think it'll be my honor to swoop into the rescue like some kind of superhero."

That gets a weak chuckle out of him. "Like a pirate captain saving his besieged crew?" he suggests.

I want to argue that historically, pirates were the bad guys. But that's really not the point right now. My boy loves his seafaring fantasy. "No man left behind," I agree.

"Or woman," he says quickly. "Or cat."

I laugh, thinking about that grumpy orange beast back at the resort. It's funny because—yes—I'd even risk my limbs for that little terror if it would make Arlo happy.

"Exactly," I confirm. "So you're not getting stranded in Bali, okay? I'll look up the address on my phone, we'll take a taxi to the embassy, and we'll get you an emergency passport. We might have to wait around a while, but if we get it sorted right away, it means that you won't be worrying about anything unnecessarily. We don't want anything spoiling your vacation, now do we?"

He shakes his head but still looks agitated. "I'm sorry I spoiled our day out, though."

Unable to help myself, I boop his nose. It startles a laugh out of him. "We can go shopping anytime," I promise him. "Today, we're going on an adventure."

He takes a deep breath, frowning as I guess he thinks my words over, then he nods. "An adventure," he agrees.

I grin. "Good boy," I praise him.

We take some time to finish our coffees, and then I insist we go find the pet place Arlo heard about. He was very eager to try and brush Jolly earlier and even though I think it's a fool's errand, I get the sense that taking care of someone else —even if that's a cat and not a person—will make my boy feel better.

Once I've treated Arlo to not only a brush but some also spray-on detangling shampoo, a couple of toys that look like feathers attached to wires on sticks, and a special food bowl with a box of canned food, he's much happier, just like I'd hoped he would be.

While he'd been physically browsing, I'd done some

internet browsing. It turns out that the actual British embassy in Indonesia is in Jakarta—the capital city on a completely different island. Before I could let Arlo see me panicking, I continued my search and quickly discovere that Bali has a consulate that basically serves the same purpose. So when I hail a taxi and we bundle inside, that's where I direct the driver.

The building itself is a pretty small white-brick structure with a terracotta roof, hidden behind a lot of trees and high gates with curved, spiky barbs to discourage any intruders. When the driver drops us off on the street, I'm almost tempted to ask him to stick around. But that's ridiculous. We'll probably be here for a while, and this place isn't a prison or anything. It's got that security so people know it's *safe.*

Still, I've seen a great deal of humanity during my time in the public eye, and people can be real shitty if they let a power imbalance go to their heads. I've dealt with my fair share of asshats over the years, and if I'd been the one to lose my passport, I'd have taken any bullshit on the chin.

But it's different now. I'm not just responsible for myself. Arlo is trusting me to un-fuck the situation, and I'll be damned if I allow anyone to make him feel bad for being the victim of a crime.

I've never felt protective like this—not even with my sister as she made it perfectly clear early on that she'd slug me if I ever tried to coddle her just for being a girl. But for some goddamned reason, Arlo hasn't been given the sense of self-worth that my family drilled into me and my sister, Camila. I can tell that he doesn't think he deserves to be here. He doesn't want to make a fuss.

I'll make all the fuss for him, then.

As it transpires, however…no fuss is needed. When we explain why we're at the gate, security lets us in without question. I sense the staff is busy, but everyone we speak to shows genuine compassion for Arlo's predicament. Soon we're sitting in front of the desk of a middle-aged motherly type with a puffy afro and impressively long and colorful nails that she uses to type like the wind as she wizzes through the red tape necessary to get Arlo his emergency passport.

"That's a fun name," she declares after Arlo spells it for her the third time.

"It's…something," Arlo agrees. I get the feeling he's not fond of his full title, even though it's the first thing I learned about him, so I'm kind of a fan.

The woman chuckles, patting her ample chest and sighing as she looks at us. "Is the double barrel from marriage?"

It takes me a second to catch onto what she means, but it's Arlo who splutters in response. "No! Um, I mean, no, it's not. Not our marriage, anyway. My grandparents on my father's side—yes."

Our new friend isn't put out, though. She just winks at me. "Ah. Maybe another marriage can fix that, then."

It's the second time we've been mistaken for an established couple despite only knowing each other a matter of days, and I know I shouldn't, but I can't help but preen.

I might only have a limited time with Arlo, but even strangers can't deny the rapport we already have.

My boy is special, no matter if I only get to call him mine for a little while longer.

CHAPTER 10

Arlo

It's pretty late by the time we get back to the Kuta Paradise Resort and Spa. I'm utterly exhausted by all the drama, but luckily for me, I have Thomas taking care of everything.

I keep catching myself feeling guilty. But whenever I do, I force myself to replay Thomas's words through my mind. He *wants* to be my Daddy and look after me. And even though I made a poor judgment call, getting robbed really wasn't my fault.

It's hard for me to believe that I'm not hopeless and a burden, having been told that my entire life. But I understand that if I *don't* listen to Thomas and keep repeating myself, then I will actually become annoying.

So I probably say 'thank you' far too much, but that feels like a step in the right direction. At least when the nice lady who organized my passport told me to take care and I said 'you, too!' that made sense for once.

Having spent most of the day at the consulate, we haven't eaten a bite since the delicious rice bowl at the market. So before we do anything else, Thomas steers us toward the dining room, where the buffet is open for dinner. He helps me pile up my plate with noodles, vegetables in a sweet sauce, sticky rice balls, skinny fries, and chicken nuggets as well as a big glass of tropical juice. I'm glad he knows I need a bit of little time and a lot of Daddying without me needing to say a word.

Thomas finds us a table on the terrace. It's cooler inside with the ceiling fans, and I almost protest, even though I know he must have his reasons. However, they become clear before I even get the chance to sit down.

"The welcoming committee is here," Thomas says with a knowing grin and a jerk of his chin. I look around to see Jolly running up toward us. I gasp and remember that the staff shoo him and any other wildlife out of the dining area when it's busy. But outside is okay.

"Jolly!" I cry, holding out my hand for him to sniff. But then for some inexplicable reason, a lump rises in my throat, and my eyes get wet again. "Oh, Jolly. I had a *bad* day."

Before I can get properly upset again, Thomas reaches over and squeezes my arm. "It worked out okay in the end, though, didn't it?"

I take a shuddery breath and manage a small smile. "Yes, actually," I agree. I hate, hate, *hate* what happened.

But having Thomas rescue me like a knight in shining armor will undoubtedly be one of the fondest memories of this whole trip.

Maybe of my whole life.

We eat our late lunch in amiable quietness. I save Jolly a couple of my nuggies and am aware of Thomas chuckling at me as I peel off the crispy coating with my fingers, but I don't care. He's not mocking me. I feel like he's almost delighted by me, maybe. It certainly makes me happy to put the chicken in Jolly's new special bowl and feed him the meat on the floor. At first, the kitty sniffs at his gift suspiciously. But then he chomps everything down with gusto as usual.

Once my tummy is full, I feel less shaky, and my eyelids start to droop. "Ah, hang on there a minute, champ," Thomas says, getting me to my feet. He picks up my shopping bag and Jolly's licked-out bowl. "We need to still sort a few things before you can crash. Besides, we're still tryna kick that jet lag's ass, right?"

I hum, not sure I wouldn't rather just fold over on the dining table and fall asleep here. But the part of me that wants to please Thomas and do as he says wins over, so I allow myself to be directed out of the dining hall toward the resort's lobby.

Of course Jolly tags along with us. "Good kitty," I say, despite the fact that he keeps twining in between my legs and almost trips me up a couple of times.

Thankfully, reception isn't busy when we approach, and both the members of staff are very sympathetic when Thomas explains how my wallet got stolen with my keycard in it. I'm worried that not having my photo ID in the form of my passport will cause problems proving who I am and stop me from getting a new keycard. But the staff reminds me that they scanned it when I arrived, so they can look at it and see I am who I say I am without having to cause any more fuss.

I'm so relieved. I don't think I could handle any more stress or forms to fill out or hoops to jump through right now. I'm still ashamed that I got myself into this mess in the first place, but the staff is so nice and echoes what Thomas said about it happening fairly regularly to tourists, so not to worry.

Besides, thanks to Thomas, I have my shiny temporary passport, which will get me back to London with no worries...apparently. I still want to head to the airport early before my flight to make sure, but that's over a week away. I don't need to be concerned about that just yet.

"Okay, so here is your new keycard," the woman behind the desk is saying to me, but I'm struck by a sudden thought as she slides it over the counter to me.

"What about the old one?" I interrupt.

She frowns at me. "Old one?"

"Is it still active?"

"Oh," she says with a smile, shaking her head. "No, it's no good now. Only this one works."

"Besides," Thomas chimes in. "They might be able to see the resort name on the card, but without this disposable wallet, they'll have no clue what room you're in."

He taps the new key jovially, but a fresh wave of shame washes through me. "Um…it was still in the cardboard so *I* wouldn't forget my room number." *Again,* I add silently.

"Ah," Thomas says, but then he shakes his head and smiles again. "But it's okay. Like the nice lady said, it won't work anymore."

I hum as I pocket the new keycard, but try as I might, I can't shake the uneasiness that's settled in my stomach.

As we walk back to my villa, I chew my lip, getting more and more anxious. Those boys were wild and obviously have very low ethics. They might think it would be funny to come and try to get into my accommodation. There's nothing stopping them from getting up onto my porch, after all. The porch where Jolly hung out on this morning as he waited for me.

"Hey, hey," Thomas says as we get to the little turn-off that leads down to my villa and a couple of others. I didn't realize it, but now that we've stopped I can see I'm shaking and breathing heavily again. "Arlo, it's okay."

"What if they find me?" I blurt out. "What if they just walk through the resort? It's all open, after all. They could peer through my windows, or…or what if Jolly is around? They might chase him or…or…"

Thomas squeezes my shoulders and shakes his head. "I've been thinking about the same thing, all right? We're not going to let any of that happen, not tonight anyway."

"We're not?" I repeat with a sniff.

He grins at me. "Nope. You know why?" I shake my head. He looks down and winks at Jolly like he's Thomas's co-conspirator, then he looks back up at me again. "Because we're going to have a sleepover at my place!"

I gasp as excitement pushes everything else aside. Never once as a child was I permitted to visit any of my school friends' homes, let alone to stay the night. "Really?"

"If that's okay with you," he says a little more seriously. "Another option is to go back to reception and see if we can't get you a different room. I know the resort is pretty full with the retreat, but we could try."

I consider what he's saying. That doesn't sound like a bad idea. Sensible, even. But then I almost certainly wouldn't be near Thomas's villa, and that makes me sad. We only have a limited amount of time together as it is.

"May we please have a sleepover tonight?" I ask tentatively. "Then perhaps inquire about a different villa tomorrow?"

A beaming smile breaks out across Thomas's face. "That's an excellent plan, baby boy." I know he's just indulging me, but the praise seeps through me like warm treacle.

"Yippee," I say with quiet enthusiasm. "Could we go to yours now?"

Thomas nods. "You ever built a blanket fort?"

I gasp again, even giddier now that we've discussed logistics. "No! Can we?"

"Of course, baby boy," Thomas tells me. "So why don't we pack you up and move on over to my place? When we get hungry later, we can order in room service. We'll feed Jolly on my porch this time so he knows where to go if he wants to find us now."

"And the blanket fort," I say, feeling my age melt away with my concerns. "Can…can it be a cave full of treasure?"

"Of course, little buddy!" Thomas cries like he's never heard such a wonderful idea in his life. "And if you like, we can play sea monsters in the hot tub and watch the sun set from the back porch."

I hug myself. After such a horrible day, that sounds like the most fun adventure I can imagine. But try as I might, some grown-up thoughts slip in.

"But…Daddy only has one bed," I whisper.

I like the idea of snuggling up with Thomas and falling asleep. I really do. I just…I'm afraid of doing *that* sort of stuff with him. That sort of stuff ruins feelings. It makes things complicated. I don't want to spoil what we have. It's already been tested so much by what happened today.

Gently, Thomas takes one of my hands between both of his. They're so big and calloused compared to mine. I really like the contrast.

"We're going to make a cozy blanket fort, aren't we?" he asks me. I nod. "So Daddy will sleep there, and Arlo can have the bed. Is that all right?"

I hum, torn between relief and disappointment that I have no right to feel. That's the perfect solution! But what if Daddy is uncomfortable? He's still limping on his knee a bit. Oh! Then Arlo can sleep on the floor!

I make the disappointment go away. If I don't want sexy grown-up times, then I can't expect us to share a bed and for nothing to happen. But the idea of sleeping in the same room still sounds really nice and comforting. Safe. Those awful thieves won't know Thomas's villa number to come sneak around and look through the windows. We'll all be protected there.

And my Daddy is saying he wants me to be little for all the rest of the evening and take care of me. His boy. How could anything be more perfect than that?

"That's amazing, Daddy!" I cry in response to his question. I punch the air with my free hand, but then I calm down and place it over where he's still holding my other hand reassuringly. "Thank you, Daddy. For everything."

I might have already said it a hundred times, but a hundred and one won't hurt. Especially not the way that Thomas beams at me.

"It's my pleasure, baby boy. Come on. Let's go get your things. We have another adventure ahead of us."

He's right. We do.

And I can't wait.

CHAPTER 11

Thomas

What a whirlwind.

When I booked this trip, I had so many reservations about how it might turn out. Of all the scenarios I ran through my mind, nothing ever came close to the reality of these first couple days. Still, if I'm being totally honest, I wouldn't have it any other way.

I wouldn't want to be spending my time with anyone else but Arlo.

It's ridiculous, I know. We only just met. But it's like I was missing a puzzle piece that I didn't even know about. He's just so earnest and sweet. Whenever he's close, I feel myself light up like there's sunshine in my heart. It's no wonder that I want him around all the time.

Even if that's at the British consulate organizing an emergency passport. Hell, I'd happily file my taxes if I could have him playing by my feet as I did them. My accountant would think I'd been body-swapped.

There's just something about this guy that makes me feel I can do anything. He's trusting me to take care of him, and that faith gives me the kind of confidence I've never experienced before. I've been yearning for it without even being sure what it was I really wanted.

I'm fully aware that I can't put too much pressure on what we have—because what we have is a fling. A holiday romance. But as he skips around the main room of his villa, throwing all his possessions back into his bags, I can't deny that my feelings are real, even if our time is short.

"Done, Daddy!" he announces proudly, jamming his hands on his hips and beaming at me.

I smirk. "Is that so?" I say, peeking into the closet where I can see at least one shirt still folded up and a pair of socks that have rolled to the back of one of the shelves.

After I've checked all the drawers, the bathroom, the back patio, and under the bed, I'm pretty confident he actually *does* have everything now. I wonder if part of him left a couple of bits lying around so we'd both enjoy me catching those last possessions for him.

Besides, it's not like he can't come back here. In fact, the sensible part of my brain keeps reminding myself that he's not moving into my villa. This is just until he can feel confident that those bastards won't come snooping around. I'm pretty certain they wouldn't bother trekking it over here, but selfishly, I love the idea of keeping my boy close while he's still rattled from being pickpocketed.

He needs his Daddy. And I need him to need me.

I wouldn't say the relationship we're nurturing here is healing something inside me. I'm fortunate enough that I don't consider myself to have suffered through any real trauma in my life so far.

Sure, blowing my knee out was devastating. I wouldn't wish seeing your dreams shattered in a matter of seconds on anyone. But I had my awesome family to see me through recovery. I still have their support every day, not to mention my former teammates who look out for me, and a huge fanbase who still treat me like a rockstar. I have purpose in my new vocation. Choosing to spend my days giving back to the community warms my soul in a way that being on the ice didn't quite reach.

But this thing...this need to be a Daddy...I'm sure it's always been inside me. A crack I didn't even realize needed to be filled up and smoothed over.

I was so terrified of opening myself up to the wrong person and having my deepest desires used against me. Now that I've met Arlo, that all seems so unimportant. Perhaps the media would be unforgiving if they knew the full extent of my kink. But truthfully, I have a suspicion that the only person who's been keeping me in this particular closet has been myself.

Well, now I choose to let myself out.

It hurts to think of the hypothetical next boy, but that's only practical. The reality is that in a week's time, Arlo and I will have to go our separate ways. I just hope that when that happens, I'll be able to look back on this vacation fondly and that being with Arlo will have made me less afraid to open up my heart again.

I grin, determined to throw myself fully into the here and now and not to worry about the near or distant future. After rescuing a sandal, another pair of socks, a stick of deodorant, and some swimming goggles, I think we are actually ready to head back out.

Seeing as we're making a blanket fort, I grab some of the bedding from this villa to take to mine, leaving a note for housekeeping telling them not to worry and to knock on my door if they're concerned. I have a feeling all the staff have been warned that there might be some pretty wild stuff going on this week, so I imagine two people sharing pillows and sheets will probably be on the tamer end of that scale.

Part of me isn't surprised that Arlo has never done this

before. From what I can gather, he's had some kind of fuckery growing up. I'm not convinced he got to be much of a kid, even when he was one. It makes my heart ache to think about it, and I also want to ball up my fists and smash something.

No one should get to be mean to my baby boy. Now or ever.

"It's so cozy," he coos as we sit on the duvet that we've laid on my floor. There's a sheet above our heads, draped over the backs of chairs, creating a tent. Between us, we've made a nest of pillows, and Arlo's stuffed animals, Chippy and Snap, are keeping us company.

"It is cozy," I agree. "Daddy will be very comfy here tonight."

He bites his lip as he bounces his seagull stuffie around. I can practically hear his thoughts churning. "Daddy sleep on the bed," he says softly, not meeting my gaze. "Arlo sleep on the floor. Daddy has a bad knee."

My heart melts. "Oh, baby boy," I say.

Before I can stop myself, I reach out and cup my hand against his cheek. He stills at that before his eyes flick up to meet mine with a shy smile. Good. I was worried as soon as I did it that I'd crossed a boundary. I know I touched him quite a bit right after he was robbed, but that was an emergency. In the quiet of my villa, it feels ten times more intimate. But if anything, he leans into the touch.

"Daddy will be fine, I promise. It's Daddy's job to look after...after his baby boy."

I frown. The urge to call him by a little name was so strong then, I forgot he doesn't have one. For a while, I wondered if it was Arlo and Arlington was his regular name, but after today at the consulate, I can see how much he hates his full name. So Arlo is for every day, and he doesn't have anything for his little persona.

Would he like one? It's only something I've read about, but it would make sense that a different name would help him get into the age play head space.

"Arlo," I say as I drop my hand from his face and squeeze his knee instead to give him a bit of space to think. "When you're my little baby boy, would you like to be called something else?"

He chews on his lip and looks away thoughtfully before turning back to me. "Like what?"

Damn. Nothing like a bit of on-the-spot pressure. "Uhh…" I say as I cast my mind around. Well, there's no harm in keeping these things simple. "How about Lolo?" I suggest, shortening the name he's already shortened.

The way his face lights up could power the whole resort for a night, I swear to god. "Lolo!" he shrieks, dropping his toy and clapping his hands. "Lolo and Daddy! Daddy and Lolo!"

I laugh and squeeze his knee again. "I take it you like it," I say, relieved.

"Yes, yes, yes!"

He throws his arms around my neck, planting a big, noisy kiss on my cheek. But then he's practically sitting in my lap, our faces inches apart, and suddenly, we're looking into each other's eyes, breathing heavily.

He said he didn't want 'any grown-up stuff.' I completely respect that. But the way he's clinging to me and trembling, it feels like he's warring with something inside. I don't move a muscle, just staying still, letting him feel and think what he needs to.

I'd be lying if I said I wasn't disappointed when he drops his arms and shuffles away again, looking down at the floor and the toys that he grabs in his hands. But I'm also pleased that he's not pushing himself to do anything he's not comfortable with.

"Sorry, Daddy," he mumbles.

"Hey," I say softly, rubbing his knee. "You don't have anything to apologize for, Lolo." I use the name both to test it out and also to gauge what kind of headspace he's in. That could have pulled him out of his age play, but he doesn't correct me.

In fact, he runs with it.

"Lolo wants to kiss Daddy," he whispers, frowning as he determinedly makes Chippy ride around on the back of Snap's fluffy shell.

My heart skips a beat, but he doesn't look up. I realize that perhaps talking about himself in the third person might be easier for a tricky subject, especially while his hands are occupied, giving himself a distraction while he talks.

"Lolo doesn't have to do a single thing he's not comfortable with," I say softly but firmly. "Not ever, ever, ever. Okay?" He nods, a tiny bit of the tension leaving his shoulders. "Okay, good. But just so Lolo knows, Daddy would love to kiss him if he ever wanted to do that."

My heart is thrumming as I admit that to him. I watch his reaction closely. He inhales slowly, hugging his stuffies to his chest, licking his lips, and frowning slightly.

"Lolo doesn't want Daddy to laugh at him."

I shake my head. "Daddy would never do that, sweetheart."

"But that's what happens after kissing and…and grown-up stuff."

My heart threatens to stop altogether as coldness washes through my body. "Lolo," I say once I've scrambled together some composure. "Did someone laugh at you before?"

He shrugs, his eyes still not meeting mine. But I think that's a good thing. He might need to disassociate if he's going to bring up whatever these raw emotions are.

"Lolo likes grown-up stuff," he announces in a surprisingly cheerful tone. "We used to play grown-up games at school at night when the teachers weren't around. Lolo liked it! It felt good! The other boys would play all kinds of games with him."

My stomach turns. I'd gotten the strong impression from things he'd said that he wasn't inexperienced. But I'd just assumed he'd had boyfriends. This wasn't what I'd had in mind.

"Were they mean to you afterward?" I prompt. I don't really want to know the answer, but at the same time I have to if I'm going to take care of him properly.

He shrugs once more. "Lolo didn't mind them laughing during the grown-up stuff. Lolo liked the other boys being in charge. He liked being their good boy. But after, they would laugh and call him names, which wasn't nice after all the good things Lolo did for them."

"No, it wasn't," I agree, doing my best not to growl. It's not surprising that teenage boys wouldn't understand that scenes with intense power dynamics would require essential aftercare. I still want to beat the snot out of each and every one of them.

But then another even more awful thought occurs to me. "Lolo...did the other boys ever *make* you do the grown-up things?"

He shakes his head vehemently, and I exhale in a whoosh of relief. "Lolo *likes* doing those things. They make Lolo tingly and floaty and trembly." He giggles and blushes. "Lolo had a friend called Chris. He was *always* nice to Lolo after the grown-up games. Chris told the other boys off for being mean, too. And when Chris left—because Chris was older—Lolo still wanted to play. But every time the boys would be mean after, so Lolo stopped." He sighs and twiddles the turtle toy. "Lolo misses those games," he adds very quietly, like he's afraid he shouldn't confess to that.

There's a lump in my throat that I do my best to swallow. My poor baby. All teenagers are horny messes. But there are always those kids—usually boys, I'm ashamed to admit—who just think with their dicks and don't care who they hurt in the hunt for their next orgasm. Hell, they were probably ashamed at exploring their desires in the heat of the moment, so they used Arlo as their punchline to excuse it all away in front of their buddies afterward.

Exactly when all Arlo needed was to be told he was good and perfect and beautiful for all the gifts he gave them. Whoever that Chris guy was, I'm thankful for him. It sounds like my baby knows that submission and kink can be good—can be *incredible.* I might not have had the chance to be a Daddy until now, but I've had plenty of fun with subby bottoms in the past. Arlo is just scared of getting hurt again by trusting the wrong person.

Boy, do I understand that fear all too well.

"Thank you so much for telling me all of that, Lolo," I say fondly as I brush his soft brown hair back. I don't need him to look at me, but I do want him to know I'm right here for him. "That was so brave. Daddy gets exactly what you're saying. You're such a good boy."

He blinks and looks at me with watery hazel eyes and a tentative smile. "I am?"

I can't help but laugh, but I also smile and card my fingers through his hair so he knows I'm not laughing *at* him. "Lolo, you're the *bestest* boy Daddy could wish for."

He licks his lips and looks away bashfully. I love the little pink tinge that blossoms on his cheeks at the praise.

"It's okay to enjoy grown-up games," I assure him in a gentle tone. "Daddy will never, ever put pressure on his good boy to do anything he's not comfortable with. But if Lolo ever wants to try playing those sorts of games, all he has to do is ask Daddy. Daddy will do anything for his special boy."

He peeks at me through pretty, wet lashes. "Yeah?"

I nod. "Daddy will love playing those kinds of games with Lolo. So much. And afterward, Daddy and Lolo will cuddle because Lolo is the most perfect boy a Daddy could wish for."

He smiles and bites his lip, looking down at his toys thoughtfully. "Okay," he whispers.

I feel myself sag a little in relief. "All Lolo has to do is think about it, okay? Daddy just wants Lolo to know that he's here if Lolo needs anything. But Daddy loves hunting for buried treasure and playing mermaids in the hot tub just as much as any grown-up game, he swears."

"Really?" my boy asks.

I nod. "They're just different kinds of fun games. Daddy loves all of them because he gets to share them with his baby boy."

He hums, sounding content as he squirms on his butt. "Thank you, Daddy," he rasps like it's a conspiracy.

My good boy.

"Lolo," I say urgently, my eyes going wide.

"What?" he replies with a gasp.

I fling my arm toward the front entrance of the blanket fort. "Don't look now, but I think there are *pirates* on the poop deck!"

He flings his arms out, shrieking and giggling as he scrambles across the duvet. "Man the cannons!" he yells. "Jolly! Take cover!"

Jolly has been sunning himself outside this entire time and probably won't appreciate his peace being invaded by our silly game. But then again, he seems to adore Arlo, so maybe he won't mind.

I understand the feeling. It doesn't matter if it's only for one week.

I'll do anything to make my little Lolo happy.

CHAPTER 12

Arlo

I'VE NEVER BEEN LITTLE FOR THIS LONG.

It's glorious.

Until now, I've only ever indulged in age play by myself, like in the bath or in my room when my parents have gone out for the night. Basically—anytime I knew I could lock the door and not be interrupted. Even then, there was always an underlying worry that someone would catch me.

Not today. Not with Thomas.

As promised, we played in the blanket fort and also got in the hot tub for a while. Daddy always has the funnest ideas and never runs out of enthusiasm. But unfortunately, it has been a very long day, and I am getting tired. So even though I grumble, I don't protest too much as we get out of the tub and dry off. It doesn't take long in this heat, even if it's the evening now and the sun is setting.

I really wanted to go down to the beach again, but Daddy said it was too late for today. I felt myself getting cranky, but Daddy promised that if we wanted, we could spend the *whole* day at the beach tomorrow.

Sometimes, it's difficult for me to remember that we

don't have to do everything all at once. I guess the freedom is just making me giddy. But knowing that I've still got the next several days off from my real life makes me feel like I can breathe properly. My regular routine is so stuffy and drab. Here everything is colorful and there's no pressure.

Daddy has a very quick shower before ushering me into the bathroom. He's got a towel hanging up for me and my wash kit from my bag is ready by the sink.

It's almost on the tip of my tongue to ask if he'll wash and dry me. I'm only a little baby, after all. I need help with these things. But I don't—this time, at least. I've never showered with anyone before, even though it's something I've daydreamed about. It seems very intimate. But the idea of Daddy washing my hair makes me want to melt into a gooey puddle.

So much has happened today already, though. That feels like a really big step to take. Besides, I could use the time alone to think.

That conversation we had just now was…surprising. I hadn't been expecting it. But it was so much easier as Lolo to tell Thomas about some of the things that happened to me in the past. Complicated, confusing things.

But saying it out loud helped me to remember some important details. Like how much I really *did* enjoy having sex. Sex is *great.*

It's just not nice if, afterward, the person you were intimate with laughs at you and calls you a slut—and not in the fun way.

I like being a slut. I don't think there's anything wrong with having lots of safe, consensual sex. But if you trust yourself with someone (or lots of someones) and they ridicule you after…goodness, that's the worst kind of empty, sick feeling.

It wasn't like that with Chris, though. It's not as if we

dated. I've never had a boyfriend, so I wouldn't know what that feels like. But Chris always respected me and told me how good and sweet I was for him, even if we pretended like we didn't know each other in public. He made the secret fun. I felt special.

But even that pales in comparison to how good Thomas makes me feel. My first *real* Daddy. I thought I'd be terrified to open up to someone on this trip—and that was if I even met anyone I liked. However, I kind of just fell into Thomas's lap somewhat literally, and it's been like a dream ever since. Part of me worries that it's too good to be true.

The other part of me knows one should never look a gift horse in the mouth. I need to appreciate something rare and precious while I have it.

By the time I get out of the shower, dry off, and dress in my jammies, I'm feeling more centered and back in my own age again. There's a temptation to cling onto little headspace all the time. But Thomas is right. I can be little again tomorrow, just like we can go to the beach again tomorrow.

"I hope you don't mind," he greets me as I come out of the bathroom and hang up my damp swim shorts. "But I ordered room service for us. It was getting late, and I didn't know how long it would take for them to deliver it."

"Oh, wonderful," I chirp with a grin. The feeling of being taken care of seeps through me even more than the hot water from the shower did. "That was good thinking. What did you order?"

"Curry. I hope that's okay?"

I nod. As much fun as it is eating food intended for little palates, sampling local cuisine is actually very important to me. "Yummy!" I declare.

The food arrives not long after that, and we eat on the patio as the chairs inside are still very much being used as load-bearing walls in our blanket fort. But I think it was the better idea to sit outside and watch the last of the sun set over the jungle and the ocean as we eat.

The curry is apparently a classic Indonesian blend—yellow from turmeric, spicy, but also rich from coconut milk and cashew nuts. It's accompanied by fluffy white rice and some crunchy crackers. We wash it down with tropical juice. I could have enjoyed some wine after the day we've had, but I love that Thomas maybe didn't know what kind of head space I'd be in and didn't want to make things too grown up.

There's always tomorrow night for wine and other grown-up things.

After I've eaten all I can, there's no more fighting the bone-deep jet lag that's weighing me down. Thomas insists on tidying up our plates so I can go brush my teeth, but before I do, I open up a can of food for Jolly and put it in his new bowl that we cleaned after lunch.

"Here you go, baby," I coo at him as I place it down on the decking.

He sniffs at it like he did the last time at the restaurant. I was worried that he'd only like fresh meat and wouldn't be interested in the more processed stuff. But I stifle a little gasp as he plunges in, gobbling down the chunks in gravy with gusto.

"If you were my kitty," I whisper to him as he eats, "I'd buy you the very best food and brush you every single day." He licks his lips and looks up at me. I like to imagine he knows what I'm saying.

I'm aware it's going to be tough to say good-bye to him in a week. At least Thomas can text so we can still talk if we want to. But I assure myself that while I'm here, I can do my best to take care of this feisty wild kitty.

There's a strange sort of electricity between Thomas and me as we take turns brushing our teeth. Part of me wonders if I overreacted by not wanting to sleep in my own villa. But one look outside at Jolly and the image of those rowdy boys jeering as they ran away flashes through my mind.

No. They know so much about me from my passport, like my name and birthday, but at least that doesn't have my home address on it. The fact that they know the resort name and my villa number is just too unsettling.

Like Thomas suggested, I might go back to reception tomorrow and see if I can transfer to a different room. For tonight, though, staying here is the safest option.

Still, it's a pretty intimate thing to do with someone you've only known for a couple of days. I slept in shared dorm rooms when I was younger, but I've never shared one-on-one. I've certainly never slept in a bed with anyone.

Thomas tucks me into his bed and turns out the lights. I chew my lip as I watch in the dim moonlight as he fusses with pillows and blankets, my thoughts a hurricane in my head.

I want to protect myself. But when we talked earlier, Thomas made me feel *so* safe.

"Daddy?" I say, sitting up in bed and clutching the duvet to my chest.

"Yes, baby boy?" he replies in the near darkness.

I take a breath and give myself a moment to back out.

I don't want to.

"Daddy come sleep in Lolo's bed."

There's a pause. I deliberately used my new little name to tell him what I want—or what I don't want. Not yet, anyway. I'm not ready to be intimate. But I'm not having him throw his back out by sleeping on the blasted floor, either.

"Lolo," he says carefully, but I'm beyond tired, and he doesn't have to worry about this anymore.

It's easy to regress as I shake my head, even though he probably can't see much more than a lump on the bed. "It's bedtime, Daddy!" I cry, slapping the mattress beside me.

"Come sleep now! We're going to count flying fish until we go night night."

He chuckles. "Is that right?"

"Yes, Daddy," I say smugly. Then I can't help but yawn. "Bedtime now. Lolo sleepy."

I hold my breath and start counting. But before I can get to ten, he starts extracting himself from the blanket fort, making his way over to the other side of the bed. I release my breath and grin, throwing the duvet back for him.

"Yay! Thank you, Daddy."

"Thank you, Lolo," he murmurs back, slipping between the sheets.

With the ceiling fan spinning lazily overhead, it's cool enough to snuggle under the covers and not get uncomfortable. But Thomas is radiating heat, even while wearing boxers and a T-shirt. I'm so ridiculously hyperaware of him, so much so, I don't want to move and make the mattress bounce.

He chuckles again. "Relax, baby boy," he tells me. "Take a deep breath and get comfy for Daddy."

I'm glad it's dark so he can't see my sheepish expression. I insisted he get into the bed with me, then immediately freaked out about it. But I do what he says and inhale before squirming around to settle on my side. It's slightly easier with my back to him, like there's a tiny wall separating us.

"Night night, Daddy," I whisper.

"Night night, good boy."

I beam, even with my eyes closed, his praise filling me up until it spills over everywhere. It's easy to let go and fall into unconsciousness when I feel like I'm floating on these feelings.

———

After everything that happened, it's not so surprising that I have more of a lie-in the next morning. I'm heavy with sleep. If I roused during the night, I don't remember it. But I must have moved at some point.

Because I know I fell asleep with my back to Thomas and now I'm facing the other way. As I blink my eyes slowly open, fumbling my way into consciousness again, I see that he's also facing me.

He's watching me.

He bites his lip as he realizes I'm waking up, but as soon as I see him, I smile. His hair is glowing like a halo around his head in the early morning sunshine. That would make sense, seeing as he's my angel and all.

"Hello," I rasp.

Admittedly, if it were anyone else, I'd be spooked at being watched while I slept. But this is Thomas. I trust him, and I'm relieved when he stops looking worried and starts smiling back at me, too.

"Hey, baby boy," he says, his voice all sleepy and warm. "You okay?"

I nod. The room is so quiet. There's just the thrum of the fan above us accompanying the beat of my heart.

Why am I hesitating? What am I so worried about? It's as if a good night's sleep has rinsed my brain out, taking all my old fears and doubts down the drain. I might only have a matter of days that I can spend with Thomas. Why am I *wasting* them?

There are so many unspoken words hanging between us, but I realize I don't want to talk. Actions speak louder than words, right?

So before I can overthink anything, I slide my hand down the mattress under the covers. My fingers entwine with Thomas's, my palm softer and smaller than his. Then I bring both our hands back up and nuzzle my cheek against his knuckles.

He sucks in a short, surprised breath, his eyes widening. I'll be honest, I'm not really sure what I'm doing here. I just know that I want to be close to him and that I'm not afraid.

When he tugs slightly on my hand, I let him move it over to his side. He mimics me as he rubs his scruffy cheek against my fingers, making me giggle.

"Baby boy," he whispers reverently.

Then he drags both our hands down just a fraction... before placing a chaste kiss on the sensitive skin inside my wrist.

My heart skips a beat as I forget how to breathe. This is it. He's giving me the chance to back off, to slow things down, or say no altogether.

Instead, I launch myself forward, crashing our mouths against one another, finally letting myself be completely free of my past.

CHAPTER 13

Thomas

All my resistance evaporates as Arlo throws himself against me. My hands are all over his perfect body, running over clothes and skin as my mouth devours him. Almost immediately, he opens up, slipping his tongue hungrily against mine. He's so warm in my arms, and he tastes like toothpaste, sleep, and something sweet that's uniquely him.

I hadn't realized how badly I'd been craving this, but in that moment, I know it's been ever since I laid eyes on him in the airport lounge. This boy just tripped and fell into my heart when I was least expecting it. All this time, I've been fighting the inevitable.

"Daddy," he mumbles against my lips, and I fucking whimper in response. I've been afraid this is all too good to be true.

It's time to let go and give in. Because apparently this is really happening, and I'd be a fool to reject it simply due to fear.

"Arlo," I say back, thrusting my fingers through his thick, dark hair and cradling the back of his head. My other arm snakes around his waist, hugging him against me. I want to take care of him in every way. He doesn't need to worry about a thing.

Except it's not just kissing. He's grinding against me, clearly already hard, which isn't surprising as I woke up that way having dreamed of him all night. I knew when he begged me to share the bed with him, there was a chance I wouldn't be able to resist temptation. I told myself if he didn't start anything, then I'd keep my distance and be respectful. After our conversation yesterday evening, he knew where I stood.

And apparently, he's made it very clear where he stands. Or lies, rather. He tugs at me as he rolls onto his back, yanking me until I'm hovering above him on my hands and knees.

I grin, my heart racing. "Bossy baby," I say appreciatively.

He giggles and wriggles beneath me. Last night, I very much enjoyed how cute he was in his jammies with the duckies all over them. The pocket has a speech bubble on it that says 'Quack!' I drop my head down and kiss it, touching my lips above his heart.

"What do you want, sweetheart?" I ask as I lean back again.

He's panting below me, his eyes dilated and his body trembling. Fuck, I could just eat him all up. But he needs to set the pace and give me boundaries.

"I...I..." He gasps, hands fluttering over my back as he writhes against me.

"Shh," I soothe, then press a kiss to his damp forehead. "It's okay. Daddy's here. You can have whatever you want. Why don't we take it slow?"

But he shakes his head. "I don't want to waste a single second with you," he says in a rush, his expression earnest.

Damn. I know that feeling.

Nodding, I swallow. "Me, neither, baby. Do you want Daddy to take our clothes off?"

The little puff of air that escapes his lungs along with his smile tells me he's relieved and that was the right suggestion. He squirms, trying to raise his arms above his head despite being caged by my body.

"Off, Daddy! Off!" He's humming and laughing as I kiss his cheeks and neck, skimming my hands over his lithe body, loving all his hot, pale skin.

As I help him remove his T-shirt, I see he's not so pale anymore. The blush from his face is traveling down his chest, blossoming like a flower. He's only got a little dark hair between his pecs and a happy trail on his soft tummy, leading me down into the best kind of temptation.

"What do you want, baby boy?" I ask as I press kisses below his belly button, my fingers looping under the elastic of his pajama pants, moving toward his hips and back again.

He arches his back and whimpers. It's so glorious. I know I'll remember such a delicious sight for a long time to come.

"Touch me, Daddy," he rasps. "Kiss me. I want it so badly. We can play any game you want."

"Is that right?" I'm deliberately teasing him as I mouth kisses through the material against his straining cock. He's squirming and making fists against the bedsheet, but he's just lying there for me, submitting to whatever I want to do.

It's incredible.

"*Yesss,*" he hisses before gasping for air.

I chuckle darkly, reaching up and pinching his nipple. "Are you Daddy's good boy?"

"Yes, yes, please!" he squawks.

For a second, I wonder how long it's been since he had this kind of sex with anyone. Then I decide it doesn't matter, because there's no way that those awful boys from before took care of him the way I'm going to.

I want to keep things simple, physically speaking. I don't want to waste time prepping him for penetration or anything. Besides, my condoms are in the bathroom, and I have no intention of leaving this bed until we've both come our brains out. But I want to see what kinds of verbal stimuli he likes the best.

I rub my nose against his hard length through the cotton, inhaling his musky scent. "Daddy wants to play a game with his new favorite toy. Do you want that, baby?"

"Yes, yes!" he begs, making my own cock throb in my boxers.

Here's where I want to take a chance. Like Arlo said, we haven't got a minute to waste together. So I take the plunge, hoping I haven't completely misread what he told me yesterday.

He said he loves sex. He just wants to be treated with respect afterward.

I can do that. I can do that in spades.

"Such a little slut for Daddy, aren't you, baby boy?"

He doesn't even flinch or hesitate or anything. There are tears in his eyes as he lifts his head to look down his body at where my face is still nuzzling against his hard, leaking cock.

"I'm such a fucking slut, Daddy," he hisses. "Help me, please! Touch me! I'll be *sooooo* good for you."

His moaning and wailing tip me over the edge. I stop messing around and hook my fingers over his waistband to drag his pants over his butt and down his legs. He lifts his hips to help me discard them, and I throw the covers totally off us as well as we're already overheating.

There's my boy, splayed out and totally naked for me.

All mine.

"Good boy," I mutter before dropping down and swallowing his cute, skinny cock down in one movement. He screams in pleasure, so loud it makes me grateful that all the villas are a reasonable distance away from each other.

"Daddy, Daddy, Daddy," he's babbling as he quivers under me. "So good. I love it. Thank you, Daddy. Don't stop. I love it."

I play with him for a while, but I don't want him to come just yet. When I pop off, he cries out and whimpers, but I capture his pouting mouth in a fierce kiss, letting him taste himself.

"Do you want to suck on Daddy's cock, you little slut?"

He digs his fingers into my flanks and tries to rut his cock against mine which is tented obscenely in my underwear. "Fuck, Daddy! Yes, please. Please let me!"

We're still kissing messily, but I break away just for a second to whip off my T-shirt, then mumble my words against his lips. "Are you going to be a good boy for Daddy and take his cock?"

"Yes, yes!" he yelps.

"Are you going to lie back and let Daddy fuck your pretty, slutty mouth?"

He mewls and nods as I lean back. It's easier to quickly stand up and shove my boxers down, but I don't hate the way he drinks my body in with wide, wet eyes.

"Daddy, you're *so* hot," he moans, almost like it's a bad thing. I drop my head back and laugh before crawling over him again. He runs his hands over my body—darker, thicker, and hairier than his own. "So fucking hot."

I capture his bottom lip between my teeth, dragging it through before releasing it. "Such a slutty potty mouth," I admonish. "Daddy needs to shut it up."

"Yessss," he practically howls as I move up the bed.

For a second, I just rub the fat tip of my cock against his swollen lips. He's lying there with his head on the pillow, hands on either side of his head as he stares up at me with spiky lashes, his breaths ragged.

"Jesus Christ, you're gorgeous," I utter, reveling in the moment a little longer. "My perfect baby boy."

"Daddy," he whispers, then gives my dick a saucy little lick, capturing the dripping precum.

"Fuck," I grunt, pushing my length past his lips, feeding him until he can't take any more. When he splutters, I almost withdraw in a panic. But he grabs two handfuls of my ass and holds me there, breathing heavily through his nose as he slides the head of my cock down his throat.

And *swallows.*

"Shit! Fuck!" I bellow.

Our eyes lock. Now that he's got me where he wants me, he's stopped moving. He even drops his hands back down by his head, fluttering his eyelashes as he swallows again.

I asked if I could fuck his mouth.

He said yes.

I'm careful at first. I don't know his body well enough yet, so I need to test his limits. But wow this boy *is* a slut. He knows exactly how to drive me wild as he takes me deep, and from the delicious moans coming from him, he's loving every second of it.

Lucky me.

I watch my length sliding in and out of his beautiful mouth. I could come right now, but I don't want that just yet. I grit my teeth and enjoy the gift he's giving me for as long as I can stand. But then I have to pull out before I ruin everything.

He gasps for air. I let him catch his breath as I scoot back down the bed, aligning our bodies so our cocks line up. I kiss his neck as I wrap my hand around us both, vigorously stroking our slippery dicks against each other.

"Come for me, baby boy," I growl into his ear, nipping at the lobe. "Come for Daddy. I know you can. My good boy."

He arches his back, screwing up his face and scratching my back, and he starts spurting all over me. It's all I need to release myself, my vision blacking out for a second as the orgasm rips through me.

When I regain my senses, I gasp for air just like Arlo did, gathering him in my arms and hugging him tightly to me, not caring about the sticky mess between us. Actually, I love that the evidence of our tryst is painted all over our bodies.

"Oh, baby," I grunt, planting kisses all over his face and hair. "Arlo, sweetheart. That was so perfect. You were so good for Daddy. Did you like that?"

When he doesn't answer, I lean back to look at him.

He turns away from me, tears streaming down his cheeks.

My heart *drops.* "Baby, no," I rasp, utterly horrified. "What's wrong? Are you okay?"

He shakes his head, making me even more worried, but then he's pawing at my back and hugging me again, tucking his face against my neck.

"That was *amazing,* Daddy," he utters between sobs. "I'm sorry. I've got too many feelings. But I loved it! It was amazing. Don't go anywhere. Please stay."

Relief crashes through me harder than the orgasm. I hug him with everything I have, rolling us onto our sides so we can lie together. "I'm right here, baby boy," I assure him. "I'm not going anywhere. Daddy's going to take care of you because you're beautiful and perfect and…and…"

"And a little slut?" he asks shyly, peeking at me through wet lashes, a hint of a smile on his lips.

"The bestest, sweetest, loveliest slut," I tell him.

He dissolves into giggles that are still punctuated by the occasional hiccuping sob. I can appreciate he's probably got a lot going on in his head right now.

But I keep my promise. I don't move an inch. I keep him wrapped up in my arms as he slowly comes down from his high, telling him that he's good and beautiful and mine. When he's ready, I'll get us in the shower, then see if he wants to go to breakfast or order more room service. Whatever he wants, whatever he needs.

Because he's right. I'm done fighting this. We're not going to waste a single moment of this precious time we have together.

CHAPTER 14

Arlo

"You dare steal from the Dread Pirate Lolo!" I cry, brandishing the empty plastic bottle I'm using as a cutlass, spraying sand in a circle as I spin around and face my enemy. Thomas is giggling more than cowering, but that's okay. I'll show him. "It's Davy Jones's locker for you, matey! Time to walk the plank!"

"Oh, yeah?" Thomas drawls, flicking his eyes up and down my body in a way that makes me instantly tremble. "You're gonna have to make me, Captain Lolo."

I squeal and scamper over to him, crashing into him where he's sitting down on a blanket. Luckily, we've already finished eating and packed our food away, so it doesn't matter that we kick up even more sand around us.

Nothing matters, actually, other than the fact that Thomas is kissing me again.

This morning was…well, I didn't have the words then and I certainly don't now with our almost naked bodies pressed together again on the beach. Our swimwear won't hide much if we get too excited. We're in public, so we'll keep it respect-ful. But bloody hell, I can't stop touching him, and I don't want to. His big, muscular body is pretty much what I've been imagining when I've tried to conjure up my perfect Daddy for the past several years.

Everything about him is perfect.

Somehow, from just one conversation he worked out exactly the kind of dynamic I've been craving since I first started fooling around with the other boys at school. Except he did it with the confidence of a man, of my Daddy.

And then *afterward?* I was ashamed at first at my reaction, but when Thomas understood what was going on, he seemed so touched by my honest and raw emotions. He held me and kissed me and just repeated over and over how perfect I am and how much he loved what we did together. How I was his good boy.

I'm going to be his good boy for the whole of the rest of the trip. That might only be seven days, but I'm going to make them seven days of heaven that he'll never forget because I know I'm not going to. Not ever, ever.

Before the kissing can get too wild, he settles me back down on the blanket, straightening it up around us and brushing off some of the excess sand. When he gets out the bucket and spade as well as the different shaped molds, I squeak in delight and start making various sculptures around us. We're under a parasol with palm trees rustling nearby, the turquoise waves crashing onto the shore several meters away. There are other people in the distance, but they're far enough in the distance that it feels like we're all by ourselves.

I don't know about anyone else, but this is my idea of paradise.

The only thing missing is Jolly. He followed us around all morning, first appearing on the patio as we went to go get breakfast and walking with us all the way to the dining hall. Thomas offered more room service as an option, but I thought it was probably a good idea to get a little space to think. Otherwise, I would have just jumped him again once my dick recovered from round one.

Did I mention how much I love sex? How much I've *missed* it?

Well…missed might not be the right word, actually. You can't miss something you've never had, and I've certainly never been treated the way Thomas treated me in bed earlier today. *Phew.* It's probably a good thing that I didn't know how good it could get. I would have been an even hornier mess in school.

I'm glad that Thomas gets me. That he seems to really enjoy the way I feel about sex. For a long time, I wondered if I was as much of a freak as my school chums used to insist I was.

It always left such a dirty taste in my mouth that they would love fucking me in the moment, but then as soon as they cleaned themselves off, I became a joke. Nothing but a silly slut to be laughed at.

I always knew that 'slut' wasn't a bad word, though. Ginny has always hammered that into me since we talked about the birds and the bees. Because of course my parents never *once* discussed safe sex with me. Thank goodness for my cousin and her frank words, not to mention the box of condoms she forced upon me.

That was something else the boys used to tease me for. I refused to do anything with them without protection, even blow jobs. I know the risk of transmission from those is low, and with Thomas, I trust him. But those boys were nasty, and I always stood my ground. They might have bitched and moaned about it, but at least they never broke that rule.

I realize my thoughts have run away with me. I take a deep breath of warm air and glance up to the resort in the trees where Jolly will no doubt be waiting for us to return. He stopped following us at the top of the stairs that lead to the beach as if there was a forcefield there. That's okay, though. I like to think that if he knows to remain on the grounds of the resort, he'll be safer.

In his honor, I take the stick end of the spade I was using to make castles and start drawing a Jolly Roger flag into the sand. I've doodled it a lot, so the familiar skull and cross-bones shapes come naturally to me.

"Baby boy," Thomas says in a quizzical tone. "Can I ask you a question?"

"Of course," I say. I've finished the flag, so I pat out another seashell. Earlier, Thomas fetched me a bowl of water to mix with the sand. Therefore, it's just damp enough to hold really good shapes.

"Why do you love pirates so much?"

"Because they're awesome!" I cry without hesitation. "Shiver me timbers!"

He laughs and rubs my bare back. I bite my lip and look at him, feeling all warm and tingly.

"They are," he agrees. "But…aren't they also the bad guys? You're such a good boy. I was just wondering why they make you happy."

I chuckle. "Silly Daddy. *Some* pirates were bad guys. Some people in every group are the bad guys."

Now, I'm not stupid. I know the difference between history and reality and fiction. I'm sure most pirates did a lot of horrible things in real life. But I'm talking about the *idea* that pirates represent here. That's what I love. Maybe when I'm big again, I can explain it to Thomas some more. But I'm so happy in little space right now, I try my best to convey what enamors me to them so much, using the best words I can.

"Maybe pirates aren't the baddies," I say as I focus on my next creation made of sand. "Maybe the navy is. The navy just wants to make everybody follow their rules, live on their schedule, do the jobs they want people to do, not what will make people happy."

I can feel Thomas watching me carefully. "Oh, I see," he says kindly. "That sounds pretty tough, buddy."

Nodding, I make another sandy seashell. "It's horrible, Daddy. It makes people feel sad and lonely and like the things they want to do are wrong." He hums. I think he knows who I really mean by 'people.'

"But pirates are different?" he prompts.

"Uh-huh," I agree. "Pirates are *free*. Pirates have their own rules and codes and honor. Yes, some pirates do mean things. These ones should have better rules."

I scowl, but Daddy laughs at me, so it doesn't last long. "It's good to have rules about not killing and robbing people," he says sagely, making me giggle.

"People generally frown on murder," I tell him wisely.

"So I've heard." He winks at me.

"But *nice* pirates," I continue to explain. "They don't want to hurt regular people. They just take what they need from the navy to survive. Mostly they just want to be left alone. Free to spend their days how they like doing what makes them happy. Making friends like them. Falling in love with whoever they want."

I'm aware by the time I've finished speaking, I've gotten quiet. There's a lump in my throat and my eyes feel prickly.

"Lolo," Daddy says as he squeezes my knee. "Can I ask you a question about pirates?"

"Yes, Daddy," I tell him softly.

He nods and thinks for a second. "Actually, my question is about the navy. They don't like the way pirates act, right?" I nod. "They try and make the pirates more like the navy. But the pirates don't want that, do they?"

"No, Daddy." I sniff. I don't want to be sad, but at the

same time, it's nice that Thomas can maybe understand me a little better.

"The navy wouldn't like Daddy, would they?" he asks gently.

It hurts, but I shake my head. "No, they wouldn't. They wouldn't like Lolo, either. They want Lolo to be Arlington. Arlington is supposed to be a *man.* He's supposed to marry a nice lady and have babies and run the navy someday."

I don't feel the tears running down my face until Thomas reaches out and stills my hands. I didn't realize I was smashing up my sandcastles, either. I hiccup and look at him, wishing I didn't have to think about these things.

"I wish Daddy and Lolo could stay on the beach forever," I say, my voice cracking.

"I know, baby boy." He brushes the sand off his hand before reaching up to wipe the tears from my cheeks. Then he grins at me. "Only if Jolly can stay, too," Thomas adds.

That barks a startled laugh out of me. I know Thomas is afraid of the orange beast, but it means the world to me that he'd include my adopted cat in our imaginary getaway plan.

"Daddy, Lolo, and Jolly," I agree. "Family of three. Pirates pick their own families, you know? That's their crew. They rely on each other and help each other out."

"That sounds good," Thomas says.

I hum and start remaking some of my destroyed sand sculptures. "Boy pirates can marry other boy pirates, too," I tell him, aware I'm blushing. This might be where my initial fixation came from when I read about pirates all those years ago.

"Can boy pirates marry Daddy pirates?" Thomas asks with a laugh, making me squirm. I know he's just teasing, but even talking about marriage with him makes my whole body burn with something else I didn't even know I was yearning for.

"Naturally," I tell him in a precocious tone. But then I bite my tongue between my teeth and snicker. Talking about marriage is a bit much, so I continue telling him my facts. "The captain performs the ceremony. It's called 'matelotage.' Nobody makes pirates marry nice innocent girls and force them to make babies together."

"Oh?" Thomas raises his eyebrows and smirks. "Does that mean one of the pirates can be the baby, then?"

I giggle and nod. "Yes, Daddy."

"Well, I like the sound of that," he says.

The conversation moves on after that. Thomas helps me build a moat around my sandcastle and uses some driftwood as a bridge. Then we play in the water for a while, splashing in the waves. He tickles me and makes me squeal until he quietens me with salty kisses.

I know this can't last forever. It's just an escape from the reality I'll face when I return home. There's no defying my parents, and if they want me to marry and continue the family name, that's what I'll have to do. I don't have any other options or prospects.

But I think that Thomas understands about pirates now and why they're so important. If I could, I'd choose someone like him to be my family.

At least for now, I can pretend.

CHAPTER 15
Thomas

THE NEXT FEW DAYS ARE A BIT OF A DAZE THAT BLEED INTO one another. It's possibly a bit disconcerting that Arlo and I are inseparable, but seeing as we're both ridiculously happy, neither one of us is protesting to change the situation.

Somehow, the topic of Arlo getting another room never comes up between us, and no one at the resort appears to mind us sharing. In fact, yesterday we came back to not only a made bed but also one strewn with rose petals. There was also complimentary Champagne and strawberries in the minifridge. When I asked Kirana if she knew anything about it, she declared she could no longer speak any English and ran off cackling.

Hearing Arlo talk about his troubled home life—even if it was in code—was tough. And yeah, he's obviously from wealth, but from the way he cried over his stolen wallet and a few other details he let slip, I'm almost certain he saved up all by himself to come on this vacation.

Money doesn't change the facts. When he goes back to England, sooner or later, he'll face getting married off to a stranger who his parents will pick for him that he'll never be sexually attracted to.

It breaks my fucking heart.

I've tried broaching the subject a few times, but he just smiles and shrugs it off, saying "It is what it is!" like his destiny is carved in stone.

I know it's not. I made my own destiny with blood, sweat and tears. Arlo shouldn't be bullied by anyone about how to live his life, least of all his parents. But he's going through so many new life experiences right now, and this thing between us might be burning strong, but it also feels like a fragile little bird. I don't want to push him too hard too soon.

There's a devilish, unhelpful voice in the back of my head, which keeps whispering that just because we live in different countries doesn't mean we can't still talk once we leave Bali. Before, I've been telling myself that his life is in England and mine is in New York.

But what if that's not the case? Could this thing between us have a life beyond this vacation?

Even though we're over the halfway mark of our stay, it still feels too soon to worry, hope, or push about anything like that. But maybe that's the point. Maybe we've got more time than I initially could have dreamed, and we can talk about previously unimaginable things at a later date.

One thing's for sure, and that's Arlo isn't close with his family. In fact, I'm pretty confident they're the primary assholes who fucked him up in the first place. My dad's never been in my life, but I have such a big, supportive family, I can't fathom how lonely it would be without them.

It makes me think reckless thoughts, like how I want to be there for Arlo in the ways his folks let him down. I want to stand between him and them so they can't hurt him anymore.

I mean, come on—it's insane. Who in this day and age

would marry their gay son off to a woman and demand not just one but multiple heirs from him? Is this fucking Bridgerton?

I try my best not to get mad about it. Right now, those people and their warped values aren't intruding on our lives. I just want to treasure every day I get to spend with Arlo here in paradise.

The past couple of days, we've stayed close to the resort, lounging about by the pool or on the beach during the day. We joined in with a few of the little-focused scheduled activities run by the organizers, like the sandcastle competition and pool party. Arlo got to spend more time with his new friend, Colby, and his partner, Jalen. That young man shines like a jewel, but nothing burns as brightly as the way he looks at his best friend-turned-lover.

As the boys played, it gave me a chance to hang out with their Daddy, Andreas, some more. He refrained from saying an outright 'I told you so,' but he still smirked generously at me and roped me into conversations about how great it is to be a Daddy to a sweet baby boy.

Asshole. I love it. We even swap numbers at his suggestion that I might want parental advice down the line. I wonder if he'll be able to do anything for my broken heart when I have to let Arlo go, but I refuse to dwell on that thought for too long.

At night, Arlo and I very much enjoy our private time back at my villa. Arlo's sweet body is a buffet I'm loving exploring inch by inch.

The way he loses himself in passion is one of the most joyous things I've ever witnessed. Considering the shit he went through at boarding school, I think he's remarkable for coming out the other side with such a healthy attitude toward sex. The way he responds to my touch is such a precious gift.

I feel like the luckiest Daddy alive.

Today, however, we both agreed that as much as we loved the last couple of days, we didn't want to travel this great distance and not take in any local culture. Our only outing so far ended in a minor disaster, and I don't want that to be Arlo's sole experience of such a wonderful place.

Besides, I'm still trying to take things relatively slow. Us both lying in the sun with only swim shorts on gives me all kinds of ideas about what I want to do next to his beautiful body. We've kept it to hand and blow jobs as well as frotting, but I doubt it will be long until we want to move it up to the next level.

Going out and doing touristy things in a busy area means I get a bit of breathing room to think with my upstairs brain. At least for a few hours.

We've taken a tour bus from the resort to a little temple on the coast. The ancient Hindu shrine becomes its own little island depending on the height of the tide, but at the moment, it's still connected to the mainland via a rocky stretch of land. We marvel at stunning black stone carvings in the towering gateway entrances, embellished with shining gold details. The waves never stop crashing around us, creating an overpowering soundscape that drowns out a lot of the tourist chatter.

"This is magnificent," Arlo whispers to me, looking around in awe.

I've noticed that he hasn't taken any photos since we've been here, or at least not that I've seen. Selfishly, that suits me. I have to be very careful about keeping my presence here a secret. But I'm also aware that he does too—not from the public but from his family. The thought makes me sad, but it's a necessity for us both. I'd rather be here anonymously together than not at all.

However, this is the first time I've specifically gone to a

tourist spot. The market street was different. Here, it's mostly westerners with their cameras out, making memories.

I probably should have known better.

"Oh my god!" an American voice cries out not too subtly. I wince, already pretty certain I know what's about to happen, but wishing I'm wrong anyway.

I'm not.

"Are you Thomas Beltran?" the guy asks as he bustles over to me with a sheepish-looking slim blonde girl trailing behind him. It might be unfair, but my mind immediately labels them Tourist Ken and Barbie due to their deep tans, blond hair, and brightly colored clothes. He's athletically built, and she's petite, so they fit the roles even better. My knee-jerk reaction, though, is that he's the airhead, whereas she's got a little more sense about her. He encourages my theory as he speaks to me again. "Holy shit, you *are!* Babe, look! It's Thomas Beltran!"

"I see that, honey," she says, throwing an apologetic look my way. "Are you on vacation, Mr. Beltran?"

My gaze flicks to a surprised-looking Arlo for just a second before smiling back at the couple. I'm torn between not wanting to ignore him and not wanting them to pay any attention to him when he doesn't know what's going on.

"I sure am," I say. "Would you guys like a photo?"

Ken looks like he might pass out. "Hell yeah!" he cries. I can see people around us looking our way with curious expressions. At least Ken's loud display hasn't brought any other fans out of the woodwork.

Yet.

But…that's the thing. He *is* a fan. He hasn't done anything other than be excited to run into me. I'm the one who's anxious about anyone else recognizing me, of the media learning where I am or what I'm doing.

Most of all, I'm just worried what Arlo is going to think.

"Honey, get in!" Ken says as he throws himself against my side, wrapping his arm around my waist and whipping his phone out for a selfie. But Barbie shakes her head, gently taking the device from his hand.

"Why don't I take some snaps for you?" she suggests.

I pose with Ken as he gives a goofy thumbs-up, and his girlfriend smiles fondly. I'm not sure of their dynamic, but maybe she loves this big old himbo. Who am I to judge?

"Thank you so much, man," Ken says as he flicks through the several images Barbie captured. "This has made my whole day. Wow. You take care of that knee now, you hear?"

I chuckle. Guys used to give me advice about what I should be doing on the ice. These days, they normally tell me they're sorry that my career—or, worse—my *life* got ruined. That always leaves a bitter taste in my mouth. But Ken's comment comes across as sincere. Not only that, but when Barbie and he wave good-bye to me, they both also look at Arlo and give him a nod.

Okay. So I just met some fans in the wild, and they didn't even bat an eyelid that I might be on vacation with a man. A younger man. Not that I'm old, but…well, I guess it's just reassuring that they didn't immediately point at me and yell "This guy likes getting called 'Daddy'!"

Slowly I turn to Arlo, aware that I'm wincing.

"Huh," he says, his eyebrows raised. "That was… interesting."

I hold my hands up. "I can explain."

He laughs and takes one of my hands out of the air to link our fingers together. I didn't realize how tense I was until that moment, but I relax and drop my other arm.

"I assume you're famous in some way," Arlo says. "It would explain how you could work for a charity yet also be rich."

His expression is warm, and it lets me know that he's not mad or judging me. I'm pretty sure he's just curious, which eases my worries somewhat.

"I wanted to tell you," I say honestly as I steer us into a corner where we won't be in people's way as we talk. "I just… I had to be really careful. Do you understand?"

He leans in closer with a mischievous sparkle in his eyes as he whispers into my ear. "You don't want people to know that you're a sexual deviant," he suggests in a saucy tone.

I laugh and peck him on the cheek, making him blush. "I'm out," I assure him. "As gay."

"Just not as Daddy," he clarifies quietly. I nod, then so does he. "I understand. Really, I do. You told me it was your first time trying all this out." His blush deepens. "I feel very honored you felt safe enough to try it with me, Mr. Famous."

My heart melts. "I did feel safe," I agree. "I *do*. I feel like…Arlo, I don't want to put too much on you, but I've never been this open with anyone outside of my family. Thank you for being there for me and letting me be there for you."

He looks at me with glassy eyes for a few moments before silently slipping his arms around me and tucking his face against my neck to hug me tightly. I give as good as I get, and for a while, we just stand there, soaking up each other's comfort.

Until he pulls back and wrinkles his nose at me. "Just tell me you're not a politician."

I drop my head back and laugh from my belly. "No, sweetheart," I promise. "I used to play hockey."

He thinks for a second. "Ice hockey, I take it?"

I chuckle. "Yeah, hon. Not field hockey. That's not all that popular back home."

He nods, apparently satisfied. But then a devilish grin spreads across his face. "Ooh, does that mean if I look you up online, I'm going to find lots of sexy professional photos of you?"

I laugh again, loving that's where his mind went. "Mostly me in bulky gear, I suspect," I say, tempering his expectations. "Helmet and everything. But…if you *do* look me up, the first articles you'll probably see will be about my injury."

I try not to let the sadness creep into my words. I really am at peace with it all. It's just difficult reliving that moment when I felt so helpless and out of control with a fresh pair of eyes.

Except Arlo just rubs my chest and hugs me tighter. "Daddy's poorly knee," he says sagely. "Lolo can kiss it better, later. I never did get to properly the other day." He waggles his eyebrows. "Lolo can kiss *lots* of things better."

I growl and try to push down the flare of lust that rips through me. I only manage it because there are so many people around, but I catalog it for later. "Daddy has lots of boo-boos," I say in a low, rumbly voice. "Do you think Lolo will be able to kiss them all?"

Arlo presses a finger to his chin and hums. "He can certainly try," he says earnestly.

I grin and can't help but capture his mouth with mine for a moment. "My good boy," I murmur, loving how he blushes again.

Before I can think better of it, I get my own phone out and switch the camera on. I still want my privacy. But in that moment, it feels crushingly important that I should also have something to look back on to reminisce over my time in this magical place with this magical boy.

"Can I take a selfie with you?" I ask, mimicking Ken from earlier. Arlo giggles and nods, posing in my arms as I snap a few shots.

"Send them to me?" he asks softly.

"Of course," I agree, doing it right away. "Now we'll both remember today."

He laughs ruefully and shakes his head. "Silly Daddy," he admonishes. "I'm going to remember every day I spend with you forever and ever."

I thought my heart melted before, but now it's just a puddle on the floor. I can't find the words for a moment, so I hug him closer and kiss his hair. "Forever and ever," I eventually rasp.

I'm crazy if I think when this vacation ends that I can just walk away from this boy.

CHAPTER 16

Arlo

DISCOVERING THOMAS'S TRUE IDENTITY CERTAINLY DID RATTLE me, but I was more upset that he seemed to be worried that I'd be cross. If anyone understands the need to keep your private life private, it's me. I think once he saw I really meant that, he was able to relax again.

It's obvious that he's worried he'll be painted as some kind of pervert if anyone finds out that he's a Daddy. But the truth is that no one ever needs to know what goes on in his bedroom.

It's also the truth that he's an *amazing* Daddy, and if people knew what that really meant, they wouldn't judge him for a second. I bet nobody judges those wankers I went to school with, and they were far more fucked up than either Thomas or I are.

We've shared so many secrets, I feel closer to my Daddy than ever as we head back to the resort from the stunning temple. We hold hands the whole way on the bus and all the way as we walk back to Thomas's villa.

As we reach the junction between his place and my one that I never went back to, Jolly comes running up to greet us, bushy orange tail shimmying as he bolts our way. The thing is…he comes from the direction of *my* old accommodation.

I frown and reach down to scratch between his ears as he winds between my legs. "Everything okay, little man?" I ask him, feeling his aggressive purrs in his chest. I look up at Thomas, who shrugs.

"Maybe he wasn't sure where we'd gone and thought you were back there?"

"Ohh, that's a good theory. It's all right now, though, darling. We're home. Let's go back to Daddy's place."

As I look back up, Thomas is beaming at me, making my insides go all gooey. I slip my hand against his again, and the three of us all make our way up the familiar path.

The thing is… as we approach, there's someone waiting for us.

Kirana is sitting on Thomas's porch, but she leaps to her feet as we get closer. She's got something clenched in her hands.

"Oh good!" she cries as we jog up the stairs to greet her. "I don't know where you go or…" She frowns and taps her wrist where a watch would be.

"When we'd get back?" I guess.

She grins and snaps her fingers with her unoccupied hand. Now that we're closer I can see that the other one is holding…a British passport. Huh?

When she catches me looking down, she waves it in front of my face. "Present for you!"

She thrusts it into my hands. Not really thinking straight, I turn it over, then flick through the pages.

It's mine.

I gasp, tears immediately filling my eyes. Thomas must understand what's happened as he squeezes my shoulders protectively. *"How?"* I ask.

"Did someone return it?" Thomas asks. We did file a

police report via the consulate, and they had the details of Kuta Paradise Resort and Spa, so perhaps a good Samaritan helped me out.

Kirana nods, blinking a couple of times before she grins wickedly. "Yeah, someone return it. Bad boys!"

"Bad boys?" I repeat, not quite following.

She taps my passport in my hands. "Bad boys steal from you. Bad boys come here. Kucing tell me. Police come." She cackles. "Bad boys in trouble. BIG trouble. Now you have back."

I wave my hands at her along with the passport. I can feel Thomas tensing beside me as he tries to interpret what she's telling us. "The young men who robbed me came *here?*" I ask, horrified. That's exactly what I was afraid of, but I didn't think it would *really* happen.

Kirana is still smiling, though, like it's hilarious. "Yeah, here! Your home. In hot tub! Climb like monkeys in back. Splish-splash. Kucing find me. He very angry. Show me them. I call security. They call police. Bad boys still wet when they go!"

My mouth is hanging open as I look down at Jolly, who is still moving in a figure eight around my ankles. "Jolly saw the boys at my villa…in my hot tub…and told you."

Kirana nods proudly. *"Good* boy!" she declares. "Lots of fishes for you."

"Yes, lots!" I agree, my mind reeling. "So…the bad boys are gone? The police arrested them?"

"Police, yes," she says. She puts one hand on her hip, then wags a finger on the other one, like she's telling someone off. Then she balls both hands up in front of her eyes and pretends to sob before grinning at us again. "Bad boys big babies."

"Wow," I say, too stunned to articulate much else. "Thank you, Kirana. Thank you so much."

She shrugs and moves toward the steps. "Kucing good boy. Thank you, Kucing!" She waves at us before jogging down the stairs, then heading back to the main complex.

I turn and stare at Thomas for a moment, completely wrong-footed.

"What just happened?"

He points down at Jolly, who is sitting by my feet, watching us. "Your cat is a fucking superhero, that's what happened. We should get him a cape!"

The joke breaks me out of my trance-like state. I laugh and clutch my passport to my chest. "Yeah, good luck getting that cat to wear any kind of costume."

Thomas nods grimly. "True. I do enjoy having all of my fingers."

But I agree with the sentiment and also with Kirana that my little orange hero deserved some treats. When we go inside—after I lock my passport inside Thomas's safe—I go straight to his little pile of cat food tins and quickly select the one I'm pretty sure is his favorite. Once it's tipped into his bowl, I hurry outside to put it down for him, happy when he launches himself at it like he hasn't been fed in days.

"Good kitty," I say with a slightly teary laugh.

Leaving him to his dinner, I slip back inside the villa with a sigh, toeing off my shoes and wiping my eyes. "I can't believe the police actually caught those ruffians. I didn't realize how much it was still playing on my mind, but it's like I can breathe properly again! I—"

As I finally turn to look at Thomas, I find him staring at me, his eyes glassy as he hugs himself. I immediately rush to throw my arms around him. He unfolds his to return the embrace.

"Oh, no! What's wrong?" I ask, my mind automatically lurching to the worst-case scenario. "I'm sorry they only got my passport back and not the money, but I promise I can pay you back for everything you've done for me!"

"Whoa, what? No, baby boy." He shakes his head and kisses the top of my head. "Nothing's wrong, and you won't be paying me back a single cent. I just got emotional for a sec because I can't believe how kind and amazing my baby boy is, that's all. I guess…I felt a little overwhelmed in the moment, so thankful that our paths crossed."

I bite my lip and just take a few seconds to look into his eyes. "Are you sure about the money?"

He scoffs and gives me a stern look. "What is it my naughty boy likes to call me?"

I blush. "Mr. Rich and Famous," I mumble, but he looks smug.

"Exactly. Mr. Rich and Famous Daddy likes spoiling his baby boy. So no more talk like that, understand?"

"Yes, Daddy," I say bashfully, looking into his brown eyes. "I'm so happy I met you, Daddy," I murmur.

The kiss starts out chaste, just a simple pressing of lips together. But the heat grows steadily, until we're devouring each other's mouths, fingers digging into each other's backs. Thomas starts walking me backward until the backs of my legs hit the bed. Our hands are everywhere as we divest each other of our clothes and then we fall blissfully naked onto the bed. As the rose petals fly up in a cloud around us, I realize that housekeeping has treated us again.

As usual, Thomas looms over me, pinning me against the mattress. But in that moment, he pauses to look down at me, gently brushing back a lock of hair from my forehead. "Baby," he says, that one word holding so much emotion, so much promise, it cuts straight to my heart.

"Daddy," I say back.

He probably doesn't think I see how that word affects him. Every time, there's this flicker of joy across his face, but also just the tiniest hint of disbelief as well. Like he doesn't think that could really be his name.

It is.

"Arlo, I…"

I lift my hand and touch his face. "It's okay," I assure him. That was a pretty big surprise for me today, finding out that my Daddy is so famous that he's got two hundred thousand Instagram followers. I can't imagine that what he has to say now could be any more shocking.

Of course he's not the only one who's made confessions recently. Mine might have been somewhat in code, but I don't doubt that he understood me just fine.

"I respect everything you've told me," he says. "I don't want to push you. But I want you. I'm *craving* you. I just—"

"I want you inside me," I interrupt bluntly. My eyes don't leave his as they widen, studying me. So I nod. "It's really adorable how gentlemanly you've been so far. But please just fuck my brains out. Now."

There's a pause before he bursts out laughing and drops on top of me, gathering me in his arms and planting kisses all over my neck and face before finding my mouth. "How are you so perfect?" he marvels, shaking his head and brushing our noses together.

"Because I'm Daddy's good little slut," I say, grinding my hips against his so he can feel I'm already getting hard just thinking about it.

He groans and gives me a filthy kiss. "Yes, you are," he growls before dragging my lip through his teeth.

Apparently, he was anticipating this change in direction because he's already got lube and condoms stashed away in the drawer by our bed. *Our* bed. I love that. He reaches between us with cool, wet fingers, rubbing against my puckered hole, gently forcing his middle digit through my tight ring of muscle. He kisses my lips and along my jawline, murmuring how good I am against my skin.

I hum and wriggle, loving how unashamed I am. Who decided it was a bad thing to enjoy pleasure like this? They were idiots, whoever they were. How can something this wonderful be wrong?

I've been told my whole life that what I do and the things I crave are bad. But all that dissolves when I'm with Thomas. It seems ludicrous, and the knowledge that I'm right and they've all been *wrong wrong wrong* is giddily empowering.

Thomas drops his head to suck on my nipple, leaving me free to moan about how good it feels, begging him not to stop. He pinches the other one as he nips at the one already in his mouth with his teeth. I squeal and writhe, but I make no real effort to try and escape. I love this trap I've fallen into, this exquisite torture.

One finger becomes two, but I'm getting impatient. "Da-dee," I whine and pout. He laughs at me.

"Oh, there's my bossy baby again," he quips.

"I'm ready," I insist.

He arches an eyebrow. "I think that's something Daddy should decide."

I disagree.

When I push him and roll him over onto his back, he's too surprised to stop me. I doubt he would have put up much of a fight anyway, seeing how he laughs and lets his hands fall by his shoulders in defeat.

"Good Daddy," I tell him with a smirk.

He scoffs. "Bad boy," he counters.

Nah. I know I'm his good little slut. But I better remind him of that, just in case.

I grab the bottle of lube so it's close, and rip open a condom with my teeth. Then I center myself, recalling the trick Chris and I spent so many enjoyable hours practicing. I never wasted it on those other ungrateful boys. But now it's finally going to pay off.

I position the condom carefully between my teeth and my lips, then I bend down and slip my mouth over his hard, leaking cock. He sucks in a sharp breath, but I see him fist the bedsheets to stop himself from moving.

Humming, I go lower, rolling the sheath down his length until he's all covered. Mission accomplished, I pop off and smack my lips. "There!" I declare. "All done!"

Before he can move or protest or anything, I snatch the lube up, squirting a generous amount onto my fingers. I slide them up and down his cock and then reach back and finger myself, getting the gel deep inside me and adoring how he watches me with hungry eyes as I do it.

Satisfied that I'm not going to do myself harm, I wipe the excess off my hand, then dig my fingers into his chest as I straddle his hips. Before I can reach back again, he's doing it for me, holding his rigid cock and positioning it against my stretched hole. Even with the condom on it feels amazing. With a dirty moan, I begin impaling myself, sinking down and filling myself to the brim. It burns a little but in the best way.

Good lord. I realize right then that toys are no substitute for a real-life, throbbing, red hot dick. I've missed this so much. I don't know what I'm babbling as I take him deeper and deeper, but I know I love it, and I don't want him to stop.

He's running his hands up and down my flanks as he watches me ardently. "My good boy," he's murmuring. "My perfect, delicious little slut. That's right. You're going to ride Daddy like a pony, aren't you?"

"Yes, yes, *yes,*" I hiss, bottoming out and undulating to feel him stroke my prostate like a caress.

"Show Daddy how much you love it," he rasps.

Love *it*. Love *him*. My ecstasy-flooded brain can't tell the difference in this moment.

Call me Cowboy Lolo, because right then, every cell in my body is focused on one thing only, and that's driving my Daddy absolutely insane as I start to rock slowly, pulsing him deep inside me, letting my eyes roll back as I take us both to the edge.

Daddy likes to tease and take his time, but I'm a greedy little slut. I know what I want, and I'm going to take it. I get faster and faster, hurtling us both toward the highs that are eager to greet us. He's babbling just as much as me, the two of us incoherent, bordering on delirious, locked in a cycle of telling each other of how good and perfect and hot we are.

As soon as my Daddy wraps his hand around my hard, bouncing cock, it's all over. I've been leaking pre-cum for ages, so he has a beautiful glide as he wanks me off aggressively. I'm lost within seconds, wailing and scratching my nails down his broad, hairy chest as I come all over it, thick white ropes painting my Daddy to show that he's mine.

I'm trembling as he grabs my hips, thrusting into me with new vigor. "Yes, yes, yes!" I moan despite already feeling like I've been run through a mangler. "Use me, Daddy. Come inside me. I'm your baby slut. Fuck me, Daddy. *Fuck me.*"

He climaxes with a roar, filling me up in spite of the condom containing him. Before he's even finished, he's hauling me against him, crushing our bodies together. "Good boy," he's saying with every breath. "My good, perfect boy. Thank you. Daddy loved it. Good boy. Good boy. *Good boy.*"

I can feel my heart thundering in my chest as I soak up every single word he utters. I believe him. He takes everything I give him and fucking treasures it like a precious pearl. I'm right where I am meant to be.

And I never want to leave.

CHAPTER 17

Thomas

EVEN WHEN WE'RE BACK IN OUR RIGHT MINDS, NEITHER OF US makes any mention of Arlo moving back into his villa now that those Australian boys have been caught and he'd be safe. No matter the circumstances, he's always going to be safer with me anyway. But more than that, I want to spend every second I can with him for the remainder of this trip.

Unfortunately, though, it's like time is determined to speed up on us.

Don't get me wrong, we still make the most of every minute from waking up to going to sleep. Whenever we're alone we're always touching each other, and we've made love so much I've lost count of how many times. We go on a couple more excursions, and we also join in with some more Daddy/boy activities put on by the resort. I'm pleased it gives us a chance to spend a little more time with Andreas and his two boys, Jalen and Colby, who very much enjoy playing with my baby Lolo.

But there's that word again. *Time.* It's as if it knows the finish line is near and it's rushing, desperate to cross it.

I don't know what the future holds, but I know that I'm

not ready to let Arlo slip out of my life without a fight. There are possibilities for us, I'm certain. But as our departure day looms, I can sense Arlo drawing in on himself.

No, not Arlo.

It's Lolo who I feel like I'm losing.

"Do you want to go down to the beach and play pirates?" I suggest on our last afternoon at the resort.

He gives me a sweet smile but shakes his head. "Do you think we could order room service? Maybe get some wine? Then we can watch the sunset from our balcony with Jolly."

"Of course," I agree readily, willing to jump off a bridge if it'll make him happy.

But the truth is that he's going back to a life he hates, and he seems completely resolved to his fate. It makes me sad that he already seems to have put his little self back in the box where he's lived for so many years.

I want to play pirates one more time. But it seems like it would be too painful for him now.

"Tell me how I can help," I say outright later as we sit outside, watching the last of the daylight slip away.

He sighs and reaches for my hand. I immediately link our fingers together and squeeze them tight. "Just be here," he tells me sagely.

"I'm not going anywhere," I tell him stubbornly.

We give Jolly so much food I'm sure he's going to be sick. But I don't reckon he cares, so I don't try and stop Arlo. When we head back inside the villa, I ignore our half-packed suitcases and what they mean for tomorrow.

Instead, I take my time peeling Arlo out of his clothes, spreading him across the bed, and driving him utterly insane with my lips, tongue, and hands until he forgets all about the impending journeys that await us both.

When I call him Lolo, he calls me Daddy, and all is right with the world.

Of course nothing can stop the sun from rising several hours later. I don't ask Arlo if he slept as poorly as I did, not wanting to hear the answer. I'd hoped I tired him out enough that he passed out, but that didn't seem to ease my own insomnia, so it's entirely possible that he stared at the walls and ceiling in the dark just like I did.

We leave the villa without much ceremony. I check under the bed and in all the other nooks and crannies I can think of, but this time, Arlo hasn't left a single thing for me to find. I close the door for the last time, and we make our way down the steps.

Jolly trots beside us the way he always does, glued to Arlo's side like a shadow. Arlo's crying before we even make it into the main building, so I leave him outside the front entrance while I go check us both out. I don't want him to worry about how much we spent on room service as that was my treat. But mostly, I want to give him extra time to say good-bye to his fluffy little friend before we get in the taxi I've booked.

The second I step outside, my heart breaks. He's sitting on the ground, tears streaming down his face as he gently pets the orange beast who is also sitting unusually still beside him.

"Good boy," he's whispering as I sit down beside him on the steps. "You're a *good* boy, Jolly."

I rub Arlo's back, hating how helpless I feel. "Kirana promised she'll look after him," I remind him, aware that's not much comfort but not knowing what else to say.

He nods but then he shakes his head. "I know, I know. I just…I'm just going to miss him so much."

I don't doubt he's talking about the cat. But I think it's safe to bet he's also talking about this whole place as well. What we've shared. What we had.

It's hard not to feel like it's all slipping away from us. Like a dream that naturally fades as soon as you open your eyes.

"That's our taxi," I say gently as I recognize the logo on the car that's come around the corner.

Arlo screws his face up, holding the back of Jolly's head as he makes a keening noise. "He's going to wait for us, and we're never going to come back," he manages between sobs.

"Oh, baby," I say, wrapping my arm around his back, just holding him as he shakes.

When the cab pulls up, I reluctantly let him go so I can greet the driver and help with putting our luggage in the trunk. Then I have the awful task of telling my baby boy that it's time to leave.

"I know, I know," he whispers again, nodding as he strokes Jolly's back and scratches between his ears one last time. "You're the captain now, Jolly," he tells the cat. "Stay safe."

All of a sudden, he wrenches himself away, jumping up and scrambling into the back of the car. I take a deep breath and reach down to let Jolly sniff my fingers the way Arlo taught me to do so I wouldn't spook him.

"You're all right for a hell beast," I tell the little guy. "Arlo's right. You're in charge now. Kirana will make certain you stay fat, I'm sure. Take care of yourself."

Jolly licks the backs of my fingers with his scratchy tongue. It's the most affection he's ever given me, and my heart swells.

When I get in the taxi, Arlo is hugging himself, trying to keep it together. The driver gives me a sympathetic look, which I appreciate. I meet his eyes in the rearview mirror and give him a nod.

I don't want to, but it's time for us to go.

Kuta Paradise Resort and Spa vanishes from sight far quicker than I'd like. I hug Arlo to my side for the entire drive back to the airport. He gradually calms himself, blowing his nose on a tissue I give him, and then only sniffling a little by the time we arrive.

"He'll be okay," he whispers more to himself than to me as our driver jumps out to unload our bags.

"He will," I assure my boy. "That cat is a fighter."

We all are.

We're all going to be okay.

My flight is a couple of hours after Arlo's, but there's no way I'm not going to check in with him and stay by his side until the last second before boarding. I also want to make sure there's no trouble for him at passport control after everything he went through. But seeing as he has both his passport back as well as the emergency passport, everything goes through pretty smoothly.

Once we're free of our luggage, I wander through the duty-free shops with him. When I spy a magnet with the temple on it that we visited, I immediately buy two, handing him one without needing to say anything.

Something to remember me by.

Like I could ever forget my sweet boy.

We sit in the lounge for a while, taking advantage of the calmer atmosphere and complimentary food and drink. I only really get him to nibble on a cracker, but it's something at least.

"Arlo," I say, aware that time is still slipping away from us like sand through an hourglass. He looks at me, eyebrows raised. "I would like to still talk to you when we're both home."

He offers me a small smile, but it's sad. "I'd like that, too."

"But?" I say, sensing there is indeed a 'but.'

He shrugs. "But my parents have their plans, and nothing's going to change that."

I've spent the entire vacation not pushing too hard. But

that's over now. "Why?" I ask bluntly. "You're your own person. They shouldn't get any say on how you live your life."

I want to tell him if it's money he's worried about, then he shouldn't because Daddy will take care of him. But a sensible part of my brain clings to the wheel and reminds me that we've only known each other less than two weeks. He shouldn't make massive financial decisions based on something that, in the cold light of day, could have just been a summer fling.

Every cell in my body argues that's bullshit and what we have is the start of something long and beautiful. But I have no way of knowing that.

Only time will tell, the infuriating thing that it is.

"I've been destined to inherit the family business since I was born," he says flatly. "I have my part-time job, but my entire fortune is tied into the business and the estate. I literally don't know how I'd leave or survive on my own. I'm not really good at anything." He gives a rueful chuckle. "Not that I'll be any good at running the bloody business, but at least the family reputation will be intact."

I think that's all a crock, but now ain't the time to press it.

"You're good at lots of things," I insist. "You're kind and funny and good at taking care of people and animals. And with your family business stuff, nothing's set in stone yet. Just promise me you won't be a stranger. That you'll keep in touch so I'm in the loop."

He hums, then glances at one of the displays dotted around the room. "Oh, I'm boarding," he says flatly.

That's not a 'yes.' I'm anxious as we collect up our things, but I feel like I've already pushed him too far, and I don't want us to part on bad terms.

I don't want us to part at all.

There's not much I can do to fight it, though, as I escort him to his gate. We don't talk, reality hanging heavily between us. When we arrive, people are still sitting around, waiting for their group to be called forward. He's in economy, so he'll be in the last one called. I feel like my heart is in my throat and my feet have pins and needles.

I've never felt so anxious or out of control before in my life. Not before a game or when I got my injury or when I was waiting for the approval to start my charity organization. Nothing has ever felt more important than making sure I cling on to Arlington Hythe-Wandsworth.

My Lolo.

Still, as the voice comes over the intercom calling for the final group to board, it feels like a nasty shock, and my insides lurch.

"Arlo," I say, grabbing his shoulders.

He scoffs fondly, putting his hand in his pocket. "Don't worry. I've got it this time." He waggles his passport at me.

Not knowing what to do with all the emotions overwhelming me, I drag him into a fierce hug. "I'll always be your Daddy," I blurt against his ear.

He squeezes me tighter. "I know," he whispers back.

But then he's pulling away from me and picking up his bag. He's in the line, passport, emergency passport, and boarding pass ready to show. He's speaking to the ground crew. He's moving beyond their desks. He's heading to the gangway.

He turns and gives me a small, sad wave, the ghost of a smile on his lips.

And then he's gone.

My baby boy is gone.

CHAPTER 18

Arlo

IT'S BONKERS HOW EVERYTHING CAN BE EXACTLY THE SAME when everything has also completely changed.

It's still the same house I grew up in. I've known these corridors my whole life. Yet right now, they feel alien, even though I could walk through them with my eyes closed.

I blame the jet lag for the fact that it takes far too long to realize it's *me* who's managed to come back from Indonesia as a completely different person.

It's not surprising that there's no one around to greet me after I've been away for almost two weeks, but that's okay. I don't really feel the need to talk to anyone just yet. I slept for most of the flight, but I still feel horribly groggy and disoriented, so as soon as I make it to my room, I hop into my shower, making it good and hot.

I dress in fresh clothes more appropriate for the English climate. It's true that we get incredibly hot days with high humidity, which can be unbearable without air conditioning. Most homes don't have that, especially not historical estates like here. But today it's gloomy and breezy, meaning I put jeans on for the first time in a couple of weeks.

I almost walk out of my room, leaving my opened cases a mess on my bed and my floor. But then I think of Thomas. He'd want me to tidy up after myself.

It's difficult to swallow around the lump that rises in my throat. I'm trying so desperately not to think about the Daddy I left behind. He probably hasn't even landed back in New York yet, but I deliberately haven't checked. If I do, I'll go down a rabbit hole, obsessing about where he is in the world.

How can it be that when I was last in this room, I wasn't even aware he existed? Now it feels like my heart has been cleaved in two, and the missing half is beating somewhere over the Atlantic Ocean right now.

Refusing to cry despite being exhausted and wrung out, I grab the nearest pair of socks and lob them into the drawer where they belong.

"Good boy," I imagine Thomas saying.

Smiling to myself, I gradually unpack every single possession and find new homes for the few items I let him buy me when we were out there. The last thing I take out of my pocket is the magnet of the Hindu temple that Thomas bought me at the airport. I briefly clasp it to my chest and close my eyes, picturing the way Thomas kissed me in front of everyone as the waves crashed all around us.

Then I take a deep breath, open my eyes, and slide the magnet under my pillow to keep it safe.

Eventually, I find my mother in her study. I didn't expect her to make a fuss that I'd returned, but there's still a tiny part of me that was hoping for a miracle. Other people's parents care when their children leave the country, I'm sure. I should probably just be grateful that she didn't care where I was so I was able to escape to Asia for as long as I did.

"Oh, there you are," she says with raised eyebrows and a

clipped tone. "I was wondering where you'd gotten to. How was the conference?"

I keep my smile fixed in place, even as I draw a complete blank as to what I'd lied about the imaginary conference being for. "Fine," I say cheerily. Chances are that she won't be interested in any real details anyway.

Sure enough, she segues a different topic. "Meet anyone interesting?"

She laces her fingers together and peers at me over her black-framed glasses. I think they look too harsh with her ash-blonde bobbed haircut, but that's probably why she likes them so much.

I shrug noncommittally. "A couple of people," I say in response to her question, thinking of Kirana, Jolly, and of course Thomas. "No one you know," I add, anticipating her follow-up question.

As predicted, that makes her interest vanish. If they were worth knowing, she'd already be acquainted, after all.

"It's good you're back," she says, changing the subject once more as she rises to her feet. "Your father and I have been discussing your role in the company. It's high time you became more involved, so you'll be starting your new position in two weeks' time, ready for the start of next quarter."

I blink a couple of times. "Uh…okay. But I already have a job—"

She waves her hand dismissively and strides past me into the corridor. I know better than to do anything other than follow her. "That little online thing? Oh, your father sorted all that out."

"Meaning?" I ask, trying not to sound as irritated as I feel. Good lord. I've only been back on English soil for a couple of hours.

"Meaning they were more than happy to let you go with immediate effect," she says, and my stomach drops. "Honestly, I'm not sure why you were even messing around there in the first place when you had a perfectly respectable position waiting for you with us on a much bigger salary."

My jaw drops open. "You got me *fired?*"

She titters a laugh. "Oh, you silly goose. As if it was a real job in the first place. Come on now, Arlington. You're a grown man. It's time to start acting like it."

By jumping through every hoop my mummy makes me? I think savagely. I don't risk angering her when I've only just returned home, so I grit my teeth for a second and dig my fingernails into my palms.

"Right," I say eventually, although she is already walking into the kitchen with purpose. Apparently, my response wasn't a requirement.

"You're free next Saturday, aren't you?" she says as she opens the fridge and retrieves a bottle of mineral water with a stick of cucumber in it. Just looking at it makes my mouth feel slimy.

"Uh, I guess?" I should check my calendar, but the truth is that now my holiday is over, I know how painfully open my schedule is.

She unscrews the top of the water bottle and takes a long gulp, her neck like a heron's eating whole, live fish. After daintily licking her lips, she smiles at me, although it doesn't meet her eyes.

"Wonderful. We're hosting the Madgwick charity gala this year. You'll need a new suit, obviously."

"I have lots of suits, Mummy," I say. She ignores me, naturally. Heaven forefend I don't show up to somewhere in a brand new custom-made three-piece suit that looks exactly the same as the dozen others I have in my wardrobe.

"Maryanne Sibson will be there," Mummy says, locking eyes with me and flicking a brow as if daring me to defy her. "I expect you to pay her the attention she deserves."

I dig my nails into my palms again. The attention she *deserves* from me is none. That girl is an insufferable snob. Racist, homophobic, allergic to poor people. If Mummy thinks…

Oh. Oh *no*. What *does* Mummy think?

"Why should I spend any time with Miss Sibson?" I ask, dread already pooling in my guts.

Mummy huffs like I'm being difficult on purpose. "She is a beautiful girl from a respectable family with many interesting hobbies as well as an already promising career as a paralegal. Why wouldn't you want to spend an evening in her company?"

I clench my jaw, knowing full well that she's not just angling for a single evening.

She's got wedding bells ringing in her ears.

"Of course," I say stiffly with a smile that probably doesn't fool her but lets her know she's won this round for now. It's her and Pa's house, after all. Her rules are absolute.

But she can't actually *make* me spend the whole evening with that awful girl, nor can she make me marry her. Not really.

Right?

Before Bali, I would have said that I wouldn't be able to survive without my parents. It's not just that I'm financially dependent on them, but I'm also clueless as to how the real world works.

Except spending over a week with Thomas has taught me so much. Yes, I know I'm still sheltered. But I also know that something terrible can happen and I can survive. That life will go on, even if disaster strikes. That I have my own opinions when I'm given the room to breathe.

It doesn't mean I'm not afraid of what power they do still have over me…or should I say…the power I *let* them have over me. I want to believe I'd have the strength to fight them on something as ludicrous as them bullying me into marrying a woman. *Especially* someone as terrible as Maryanne Sibson. But I'm not sure.

I need backup. Of course the person I really want to speak to is Thomas, but even if he's not still up in the air, I'm not sure if I should be messaging him or not.

I know who else also always has my back, however.

When Mummy loses interest in me, I exit the kitchen as quickly as possible before she can change her mind, my phone already in hand.

ARLO: She's trying to marry me off. Genuinely, this time.

I watch my screen, waiting to see if my cousin is around. The ticks go blue, and the dots start to bounce, so I smile in relief.

GINNY: You always say that.

GINNY: Welcome home BTW. How was the debauchery?

I roll my eyes as I wander into the conservatory, finding my favorite armchair underneath the branches of a large potted tree. It's not the same as the beach in Bali, but it's nice all the same.

ARLO: This feels like she means it this time. She's setting me up with Maryanne Sibson.

I've barely pressed send before my screen lights up with her incoming video call. I wonder if I should go and lock myself in my room rather than risk being overheard. But I'm too tired to move from the jet lag and definitely too tired of having to hide who I really am all the time.

I hit the green answer icon.

"Maryanne fucking Sibson?" Ginny hisses, looking alarmed.

It's nice to see her pale face with her choppy black hair, purple lipstick, and silver nose ring. Gosh, my parents really do hate everything about her, which is why she's so brilliant.

"She's a trollop *and* a bore," Ginny continues to rant. "I'm not entirely sure how one manages to do that, but Maryanne Sibson does. If you're going to sleep with half of Eton, at least be fabulous with it."

I giggle at how mad my cousin is on my behalf. "I know, she's awful," I assure her, pressing my finger to my lips to tell her to keep it down. "I'd never marry her in a million years. But I think it shows that Mummy is upping her game."

Ginny frowns. "How many times do I have to tell you that you don't have to entertain any of her nonsense? You're a grown man."

"No, I'm really not," I grumble.

Ginny's eyes light up. "Forget about Maryanne fucking Sibson. I want to hear all your *real* gossip. How was the holiday?"

I take another look around to make sure I'm still alone. A light rain has started to fall, and the gentle drumming on the conservatory is soothing. Which is good because I immediately feel like I want to cry.

"Oh, Ginny," I whisper, trying to hold back tears, which is difficult with jet lag kicking my arse.

Her eyes go wide in alarm. "What? What is it? What happened? Do you need me to come over?"

I shake my head and manage a weak laugh. "I mean, you're always welcome to come over. Mummy got me fired, so I'm unemployed and have plenty of free time now apparently, but that's a different story."

"Yes, yes, it is," she rasps, scowling at me. "Did someone hurt you at the retreat? I'll kill them."

I laugh again and wipe away the couple of tears that escape down my cheeks. "No, just the opposite. Well, I did get pickpocketed, and there was the whole deal with the consulate, but—"

"Stop with the side quests, Arlington, or I'm going to reach through this phone and strangle you."

"I think I'm in love," I blurt out.

I'm not sure who's more surprised. Me or her.

"Oh, wow," I say with a sniff, feeling giddy. "Yeah. I think I fell in love, and I didn't even get the chance to tell him."

She shakes both her head and her phone. "Back up. From the start, please. Tell me what his name is, and take it from there."

I rub my face, cleaning myself up a bit as I take a deep breath. "His name is Thomas," I say softly.

My heart is heavy, but I can't help but smile as I tell her all about how my Daddy and I kept accidentally running into each other until we gave in to destiny and decided to spend all our time together. How we were brave and opened our hearts to each other. How leaving him and Jolly behind nearly shattered me into a million pieces.

"And?" Ginny asks once I finish.

"And what?" I repeat, confused. "And then I went to Mummy's office, and she informed me of her plans to marry me off for the price of some magic beans."

She gives me a dangerous scowl that makes me squirm even through the camera.

"*And* what happens with Daddy Thomas next?" she hisses.

I blink, my heart sinking. "And he's probably landed back in New York by now, I guess."

For a second, I wonder if the call has frozen. But then she scowls even *harder* at me. "You know that flying contraption you just got off? It's called a plane. They have ones just like it that fly between England and America. They've been doing it for a few years now."

I scoff and roll my eyes. "I know that," I say defensively. "But honestly, I don't know what good visiting will do. Ultimately, he'll still live there, and I'll still live here. Mummy and Pa have expectations of me."

"Like Maryanne fucking Sibson?" Ginny drawls. "Arlo,

when are you going to understand that your parents can boss you around all they like? They can have all the expectations of you they want. They can't stop you from being who you are or living your life or *getting on a plane to New York.* If they did, that would be kidnapping, and the police would have a few things to say about it."

I give her a weak chuckle. Normally, this kind of talk from her would bounce off me. I've been the company and family heir my entire life. I have responsibilities. I can't remember a time that wasn't drilled into me.

But now…now it feels like maybe twenty percent of what she's saying might be sinking in. Perhaps even thirty.

"They'd be furious if I disobeyed them," I say quietly.

She raises her eyebrows. "And would you really care?"

I open my mouth. Nothing comes out.

"Exactly," she gloats.

"I don't want to be a bad person," I counter.

"You're not," she says hotly. "I just watched you crying over a stray cat you spent ten days feeding, for fuck's sake. You're kind and generous, hun." Her words echo Thomas's, and I can't help but smile a little.

"Thank you."

She sighs. "I'm going to be blunt. Are you ready?" I nod. "Your parents don't respect you, so why should you respect them?"

I chew my lip. That's so harsh but…I guess it's true. I stopped trying to impress my parents back in school when I realized that nothing I did was ever good enough. Yet I still jump through every hoop they hold up for me, still desperately hoping for a pat on the head or a 'good chap' compliment.

Am I really willing to burn my whole life down and be miserable for the sake of them keeping up appearances when it *still* will never, ever be enough?

"I hear you, I promise," I tell Ginny. "I just might need some time to think about everything."

She hums. "Just don't take too long. Otherwise, they might whisk you down the aisle when you're not looking."

I shudder. I think I'd rather fake my death than marry that girl. Whenever I'd pictured that scenario, I'd always at least hoped for someone nice I could respect as a partner.

Ah. There's that word again. Respect.

Ginny's right. My parents don't see me as my own person with his own hopes and dreams. They see someone they want to mold into their own little pawn to do their bidding. All they want is an alpha male CEO even if they have to fake it.

I know that's not me. I always have. But for the first time ever I'm starting to wonder if perhaps I can put my foot down and say 'no.'

"Hey, gorge, my phone is dying so I better go," Ginny says. "But I do expect you to think this over seriously. And text your bloody Daddy right now, okay?"

I blush, but I nod at her. "Love you, disaster gay," I say softly.

"Love you more, disaster gay." She blows me a kiss, then ends the call.

I take a deep breath. It's still raining outside, the pitter-patter on the glass louder in my ears now that Ginny's gone. I imagine Jolly winding between my legs, cross with me because I won't let him outside in this weather. Another couple of tears fall, but I sniffle and wipe them away. He's happier in the sunshine, I'm sure. Except Bali gets a rainy season like most of Asia, so...

So nothing. He'll be fine. He's got Kirana, and he'll probably make a new human friend soon enough. That thought makes me irrationally jealous, but I have to shake it off and let it go.

I realize that my own phone is on fumes, but before I get up to plug it in, I open up my chat thread with Thomas. I don't know why I'm afraid to text him, but the idea of not hearing from him again is scarier. So I just tap out a simple message to him.

ARLO: I made it home safe. Slept most of the way. I hope you made it back okay. My bags are already unpacked.

I add some emojis to show how cute I think I am and hit send before I can overthink it. Then I get up and go to my room. Seeing as I don't have a job anymore, I'm not sure what I'm going to do with my time. But at least I can hopefully keep out of my parents' way for a while and get some space alone with my thoughts.

Once my phone is charging, I can't stop myself from lying on my bed even though I know I'll probably fall asleep and ruin my body clock. But I don't really see a reason not to right now. I fish the magnet out from under my pillow and hug it to my chest as my eyes flutter closed.

Then my phone chimes, and I almost fall off the bed to snatch it up.

It's only two words, but it feels like a whole sonnet to me.

THOMAS: Good boy.

Tears leak from my eyes again, but I don't try and stop them.

Yep. I think I'm head over heels in love, actually.

Now…what the hell am I going to do about it?

CHAPTER 19

Thomas

I MIGHT AS WELL STILL BE ON VACATION FOR ALL THE 'WORK' I'm doing. I've spent most of this past week just staring at my phone, waiting for Arlo to message me back every time I send him a text.

It was such a relief when he sent me that first message. I told myself that it needed to be him who made the first move. After that, it felt like I had permission to contact him freely. I know how much he has going on at home, so I don't want to add to his stress in any way. He's the one in control of the relationship.

Whereas I'm just a lovestruck fool, who needs reassurance that this *is* a relationship.

At some point, I want to bring up being exclusive. But if he's closeted with his family, I probably don't have to worry about him running off down to the clubs and banging the first hot Daddy he sees.

Damn, if that mere thought don't make my blood boil, though.

I tell myself that it's only been a week and the fact that we're still talking is a really good sign. But I want to make plans for when we're going to see each other again. I want some kind of insight into what our future together might look like.

We're dancing around anything to do with our actual relationship, however. We talk about our days, I tell him he's a good boy, and sometimes he gets a bit flirty and teases me. But that's it. We bore our frigging souls to each other in Bali, and now we're just friends.

I'm driving myself nuts.

It's not like he's trying to let me down gently, I'm certain. It's more that he's not sure what the hell's going on in his life, so he doesn't want to make any promises he can't keep.

To be fair, I'd promise him the moon if I could.

On the plane ride back, I really worried that my feelings would fade once we weren't in each other's pockets twenty-four seven. But when I got his text, I jumped out of my skin, my heart immediately leaping into my throat, my skin tingling with anticipation.

It's like that *every* time he messages.

So yeah. I'm pretty sure this is the real deal.

I'm in love.

Which is why I'm sitting on my hands so I don't chew them off, metaphorically speaking. I'm forcing myself to be patient. Arlo might take some time to see what the shape of this is gonna be, and as long as I'm in the picture when he does, I'll be fine with whatever he wants.

Unless he wants to break everything off because long distance is too hard, and he wants to find a Daddy closer to home.

Gah! Stop!

Logically, the next thing I want to suggest is a video call. I know he's afraid of his folks overhearing us, but I figured if he puts headphones on and lets me do all the talking, we could at least start there and see how we can progress.

I've looked at those selfies we took so much they're seared into my brain. I need the real deal back or at least the closest we can manage with an ocean between us. I just want to put him to bed, for Christ's sake. I want to tell my boy how good he is and see him blush in real time.

I want to call him Daddy's little slut and watch him jerk off.

But his safety is the only thing that matters. He's never going to relax if he's worried out of his skull that his mom's going to burst in on him. It sounds like if she even encounters a locked door on his bedroom or bathroom, there will be hell to pay.

I can't imagine having your mom as your enemy. She's supposed to be there for her kids when they fall, when they're uncertain, when they need unconditional love. I don't know this woman, so I try not to hate her, but it's hard when I can see clearer every day the harm she's causing my little Lolo. At least his dad seems to be your typical emotionally detached rich asshole. That's a bit easier to manage.

Speaking of moms...

My intercom goes off. I've been musing in my living room with the TV down low, half-heartedly drinking a beer. But the buzzer pulls me out of it, and I drag my ass up to the speaker, pressing the button.

"Mijo! Let us in!"

"Mom?" I say in confusion.

I hear my sister snort down the line. "I told you he'd forget. Hey, bozo! You forgot! Let us in!"

"We have Chinese," my mom says in a sing-song voice.

"Yeah?" I say, my heart lifting.

I did forget they'd bullied their way into coming over for dinner tonight. I've been deliberately avoiding telling them about my vacation. Okay...I've been deliberately avoiding telling them about *Arlo*. But apparently now I don't have an option.

"We got *all* the Chinese," my sister gloats. "So you gonna let us in, or do we have to eat it out here?"

I scoff and press the button to open the door. In the time it takes them to come up the elevator, I get out plates and chopsticks as well as wine glasses, because I know my sister hasn't come all this way to drink juice. I hear the excited chattering from out in the hall, so I jog over to open the door before they can knock.

"There's my little man," Mama coos as she bustles her way inside and throws her arms around my neck. She's barely five foot tall, but I know I'll always be her little man until the end of time. My heart expands as I wrap my arms around her plump frame and accept her embrace gratefully.

"Hey, jerk face," Camila says, kicking the door to my condo shut as her hands are full with the bag of Chinese takeout in one and—judging by the clinking sounds—at least a couple of bottles of wine in the carrier the other is holding.

"Language," our mom says with a roll of her eyes.

Cam snorts. "That ain't any kinda language, Mama," she assures her.

The next few minutes are spent getting boxes out and opened on the table, then a mild frenzy as we pile food up on our plates. I make sure everybody has a healthy measure of white wine before raising my glass. We always toast before we drink…but in that moment I realize I'm not sure what to say.

Because I only want to raise a glass to Arlo, but he's not here, and my mom and sister have no idea who he is.

Camila gives me a questioning look. "To a good vacation?" she suggests.

"Yeah," I agree, wincing when my voice catches.

Mama arches an eyebrow and puts her glass down

without drinking. "Oh, mijo. Was it no good? I know you were worried. Were you too shy? Did someone recognize you?"

"No, nothing like that," I say with a sigh. "Actually…I met someone amazing."

Camila slaps my arm hard enough to make it sting, then frowns as she takes a gulp of wine. "Then why are you moping?"

I shrug and poke at some noodles. "He lives in England, and his family is…complicated." I explain about Arlo's bigoted, old-fashioned parents, and my family listens sympathetically.

"So there's hope," Mama says with a nod, wagging an egg roll at me.

I shrug. "Maybe? There's a lot to overcome."

"Is there?" Camila asks around a mouthful of spicy chicken. "Seems like you two are smitten. It's actually kinda gross."

She winks to let us know that she's only teasing. I sigh, feeling pretty helpless. "I'm not gonna argue with you there. Maybe it's dumb to think I've fallen in love so fast or that my first relationship with someone who's, um, like me could be a serious, long-term one."

Camila has an idea about my kink. I'm almost certain that Mama just thinks I mean a gay relationship, as I haven't had a boyfriend since I went pro and got famous. It doesn't matter, though, as she's got my back either way.

"If this boy's special, he's special," she says firmly. "It won't matter if you've known him two weeks or two years. I think your heart knows."

"But…" I bite my cheek, not wanting to sound like an insecure teenager. Who else can I ask if not my mama and sister, though? "It's a bit hard to know if he feels the same if he's living in another country."

"Can't you just ask him?" Camila says with a skeptical look.

"I could, yeah," I reply. "But I'm not sure he'll give an honest answer and tell me what he really wants. He's so wrapped up in his duties and responsibilities. I don't want to barge in and tell him that his parents are assholes and he doesn't have to listen to them. But…"

"Language," Mama says on reflex. "They don't sound very nice to me, though, mijo. If you're thinking about waiting for their approval, it sounds like you're going to be waiting a very long time."

"Oh, agreed," I say with a scoff, and take a second to pop a sweet and sour chicken ball in my mouth, pondering as I chew and swallow. "It's going to take a hell of a lot for them to accept their son is gay from what I can tell—if they ever do. They seem dead set on traditional marriage and babies."

"Men can get married," Mama says hotly, and my heart aches with love for her. "Men can have babies, too! They can adopt or use a surrogate, or I saw a trans man on the Instagram who carried his own baby." She turns to my sister earnestly. "It was so beautiful, Cammy. I cried."

"Aww, Mama," she says with a laugh as she hugs her.

I pat her hand. "Arlo isn't trans, Mama. But you're absolutely right. If we wanted kids, we could have them."

"Grandbabies," she says dreamily, making both my sister and I roll our eyes.

"Not yet, Mama," Camila says firmly.

"I don't think that would be enough for Arlo's family," I say glumly. "They don't want grandkids to spoil them. They want the next family heir."

"Like Bridgerton?" Camila squawks indignantly.

"That's what I thought!" I assure her. Then I sigh and shake my head. "I am the total opposite of the imaginary duchess these people have in mind for their son. He's been trained to please them his whole life. It's going to take a lot to convince him to take a risk and be with me. Long-distance relationships are hard. I saw so many guys on the team struggling."

"So convince him," Camila says. She's got the devil in her eyes as she takes a swig of wine. "You said it's like Bridgerton? That's basically the same as Pride and Prejudice, and one of the chicks in that goes off about how the girls have to show *more* love than they might think they feel to secure a match. Obviously, this is slightly different." She waves her hand so I can't interrupt her train of thought. "But my point is, this cute little Brit might need a truly OTT gesture from you to believe that you're all in."

I rub my chin and narrow my eyes at her. "You might actually be onto something there, sis."

She flips her hair. "Of course. I'm a mastermind."

"You should send him flowers," Mama suggests.

Camila kisses her cheek. "That's so sweet, Mama. But I'm thinking *waaaay* bigger than that."

I wave a finger at her. "Hang on, wait a minute." I knit my eyebrows together as my thoughts catch up to each other. "He said something about his parents hosting a fancy ball this weekend that he's being made to go to."

Camila slaps her hand to her chest. "A *ball?*" she cries in a pretty funny attempt at a posh English accent that I very much enjoy.

"Does that sound like the place to stage something dramatic?" I ask with a grin.

She raises her wine glass. "It certainly sounds like something better to toast to! Let's get scheming!"

And scheming we do.

Lots of it.

CHAPTER 20
Arlo

"I LOOK RIDICULOUS," I GRUMBLE, TUGGING AT MY COLLAR AS I look at myself in the full-length mirror in my bedroom.

Ginny smooths the shoulders of my black tux down. "You look gorgeous," she assures me. "Boring, but gorgeous."

I sigh and turn around to look at her. "Do you really think you're going to get away with wearing that?" I ask, in awe of her bravery as always.

"It's a dress," she protests in mock outrage.

I crook an eyebrow. "It's a bright pink nineties bridesmaid dress that you dug out of a charity shop for a tenner that you've paired with red Doc Martens and a baseball cap."

I don't comment that the baseball cap is for the team that Thomas used to play for. I half want to kill her, half want to cry, and half want to send my Daddy a photo of it and tell him that not all my family hate him.

Yes, I'm made up of three halves now. That's about the state my brain is in.

Ginny snorts and twirls in her poofy dress. "The shop only wanted three quid for it. I insisted on ten. It's just so *awful*."

I wrinkle my nose. "It's so shiny. Did people really used to wear things like this to weddings?"

"The nineties were wild, babe. Anyway, your mum said I had to come to this stupid thing and that I had to wear a dress. I am complying with both of those requests."

"This is why you're not the one she's trying to match-make," I say, giving up on tugging at my attire and heading for the door. "Everyone is going to avoid you like the plague."

"I know. It's glorious," she crows. "Right, come on. Let's go get pissed for free. That's always a silver lining."

Like me, Ginny has been determined to make her own way, and that means making her own money. But I don't blame her for taking advantage of family dos like this when they happen. My parents might be rubbish at many things, but they always get in the good booze, I have to admit.

We head along the corridor toward the stairs, and I slip my hand into my pocket, feeling the edges of my Bali magnet against the pad of my thumb. It's become my good luck charm, my comfort blanket. I've never gone anywhere without it since I came home.

It makes me feel like Thomas is close by, which is a good thing because he told me that work went crazy, and his phone has been turned off for long stretches of time over the past few days.

I've missed the hell out of him.

I'm pretty sure he's waiting for me to take the next steps in our relationship. How many times has he told me that I'm the one in charge? Texting has been great, and we've swapped a lot of photos, but I need to hear his voice, soon. See him smiling at me.

Earlier, I messaged to ask if he might want to video call later when all this nonsense is done. I have a strong feeling I'm going to need to debrief, and thanks to the time difference, it should still be early in the evening for him in New York.

The message hasn't been delivered, though. Hopefully, he'll turn his phone on in the next few hours. But if not, I'll call him tomorrow or the day after, whenever works for him.

I don't want him to think I'm giving up on him. In fact, when Pa casually mentioned that we have an office in New York a few days ago, my mind started whirling, thinking I could maybe talk my way into a trip there as part of my 'getting up to speed' training. The idea of being able to visit Thomas in his home city makes me feel giddy.

As tumultuous as my thoughts are, I'm pulled from them as Ginny and I walk down the main staircase, coming into view of a couple dozen gala guests. I make myself push my shoulders back and loop my arm supportively through Ginny's as she beams at everyone, almost daring them to object to the 'misogynistic display of femininity' she's been subjected to.

I agree with her. Why can't she just wear a suit if she wants to? It's still formal wear.

My mother appears out of nowhere, her horrified gaze traveling over the taffeta poofs that make up Ginny's shoulders and skirt, the scuffed boots, and the backward baseball cap with her short, dark hair poking out from underneath. A small bag that looks like a spider's web swings from her wrist. She deliberately went hard on the black eyeliner and blood-red lips to complete the look. If someone asked if she was the front woman for a rock band, I think I could convince them they were right.

"Great bash, Auntie," Ginny cries, slapping Mummy on her arm. "Arlington and I were just headed to the bar."

She tries to drag me away, but my mother lifts a hand and cuts us both an icy glare. "I need a moment with my son,

Genevieve," she says, apparently choosing to forgo the argument with Ginny about her outfit.

"I'll get you a double," Ginny whispers not so subtly to me. I give her a small smile, then turn my attention to my mother.

"You look ravishing," I say automatically. It's true that she does cut an impressive figure in her dark blue body con dress, but as always, she just looks cold to me. Sharp. I'd never dare hug her at the best of times, but right now, she looks like an ice queen.

"Thank you, darling. I'm afraid you won't have much time to keep your cousin company tonight, however. Maryanne Sibson arrived a little while ago, and is waiting for you on the patio."

I resist the urge to roll my eyes and manage a tight grimace that could pass for a smile instead. "Once I have my drink, I'll go say hello," I promise, intending to do no such thing. I'll probably have to interact with the terrible woman at some point, but I'm not going to be glued to her side. I doubt either of us wants that. Unless something's drastically changed, Maryanne likes me about as much as I like her.

But my mother grabs my elbow and digs her nails in through my suit jacket and shirt, ignoring my protest as she begins marching me toward the back of the house where our patio opens out onto a lawn large enough to be a golf course.

"You will *not* embarrass this family at our own event. Is that clear?"

"Mummy?" I squeak. "I'm not going to do anything of the sort. But you've got to understand that Maryanne Sibson and I are a *terrible* match. She's not interested in me. I can assure you."

"That's because you haven't tried hard enough," she snips back. "I'm completely done with your selfishness and immaturity, Arlington. Your father and I have given you everything, and you disrespect us at every turn. Well, I've let you have your fun, but that ends tonight."

We stumble outside, and she releases me, smiling and mouthing hello to a few people nearby. Most of the guests are still inside, hovering by the buffet tables and the silent auction display. If anyone questions why my mother is harassing her twenty-five-year-old son, nobody says anything.

"Fine," I snap, unable to keep my anger from bubbling over. "I shall talk with Miss Sibson. But if you're expecting anything more than that, I'm afraid you're going to be deeply disappointed."

She looks at me coolly. "And why would I be disappointed?"

"You know why," I grit out.

Her laugh is more than cool. It's arctic. "I'm sure I have no idea what you're talking about, Arlington. Now stop whining like a child and take this."

From her clutch bag, she pulls out a small velvet box. I can't help but gape. "And what is *that?*"

"Your grandmother's ring," she says smugly, opening the little box to reveal a gold band with several enormous sapphires set into it. It matches her dress, which I think is weird on so many levels. But I'm too furious to make any psycho-sexual jokes right now.

"And what am I supposed to do with that?" I bite out.

She's still calmly offering it up for me to take, which I refuse to do. "Maybe not *tonight,*" she says with a titter. "But you might as well hold onto it for when the time is right."

For a second, I just stare at her, blinking slowly. "You know this is *insane,* right? I'm not going to propose to a girl I hardly know and *really* don't like just because you snap your fingers."

Finally, she seems to get that I'm serious. She clenches her jaw and glares at me, shutting the ring box and thrusting it back into her clutch. "If it will stop you from running off to Asia and acting like a little *whore*, I'll do anything and everything in my power. You are my *son,* and you will not tarnish my reputation like this, Arlington!"

My blood runs cold. "W-what?"

This time her laugh isn't cold. It's hot and nasty. "Did you really think we didn't know, darling? Of course we wanted to believe that little story you told us. But we trusted you, and look where that got us. A retreat for perverts? I was mortified. So, *yes.* If I have to arrange your engagement to make you see sense, I will. This is not a game, young man, and you *will* behave."

I can feel the tears forming in my eyes, but I do everything in my power to keep them at bay. So for several long moments, I stare at the woman who gave birth to me, and wonder what I ever did to make her *hate* me so much.

Then all hell breaks loose.

"LOOK!" Ginny yells as she comes skidding out onto the patio, two glasses of Champagne clutched in her hands. "Look over there!"

A dozen more guests come spilling out of the house, all talking over one another as they point out over the lawn. I'd been facing Mummy and had my back to the darkness of the garden. But as I turn around now, I see there are lights in the sky.

"It looks like a helicopter is landing," I say, not quite sure I can believe my eyes.

Ginny thrusts one of the Champagne flutes into my hands. "It certainly does, babe. Let's go say hello!"

"What? Wait!" my mother barks, but Ginny has already grabbed me by the hand and is dragging me across the grass. Several other guests are beside us, carefully approaching the helicopter as it touches down. Ginny lets go of me to grip her hat down on her head, stopping it from blowing away.

My heart is hammering in my chest. I don't know why I let Ginny push us to the front. I should go back inside. This could be dangerous, after all. My recent experiences have made me slightly less naïve, which is probably a good thing. But it's like my feet are rooted to the spot. I *have* to know who has the audacity to crash my parents' party in such a spectacular fashion.

In hindsight, I really should have known.

As the helicopter settles, people jostle around me, but everyone respects the invisible line we've decided not to cross for safety. I'm intrigued, but not enough to risk getting too close to one of those still-spinning blades.

As the whole thing gradually powers down, the main door slides open, revealing a single passenger inside.

He scans the crowd anxiously while my mouth just hangs open.

He can't see me in the darkness.

"Thomas?" I croak.

"Thomas!" Ginny shrieks.

"Arlo?" he calls out hopefully.

Safety be damned. I lurch forward, throwing myself at the helicopter and the man who's half climbed out of it.

"Daddy," I sob, not caring if anyone hears me or not as I throw myself into his arms, my Champagne glass dropping to the ground.

He bellows as he wraps his arms around me and picks me off the ground with the force of his hug. I can't stop myself from bursting into tears, and I melt against his familiar body, drinking in his unique scent and just generally basking in everything he is.

"You're *here?*" I squeak in disbelief as he steadies me back on my feet. My gaze skitters over his body, which is always amazing, but right now? *Whoa.* "You look incredible," I splutter.

He grins and gives me a little twirl, and my heart almost explodes. He's in a full top hat and tails with a white carnation in the buttonhole of his black jacket. "If I was going to be your date, I had to dress the part," he says with a wink.

"My date?" I repeat. The helicopter has mostly died down now, so I'm aware that people will be able to hear him if they're paying attention.

I don't care.

He winks at me. "Yeah, baby boy. I heard there was a shindig going down and you needed a date."

Before I can make my flabbergasted brain muster up a response, a vibrating body appears by my side. "Mr. Beltran," Ginny practically yells as she thrusts her hand out toward him. "Big fan, huge. So nice to meet you."

Thomas looks at me warily. "Oh…you like hockey?" he asks, glancing at her baseball cap.

Ginny frowns. "Oh, yeah, that's the thing you do. Or did, I guess." She retracts her hand and uses it to yank her hat off her head. "I'm more a fan of *you,* if I'm being honest."

She shoves the cap onto my head instead, ruining my perfect hair that I spent ages on.

Hair I just wanted to make Mummy happy.

I readjust the cap and grin at my Daddy. "She's a *big* fan of you," I repeat with a wink of my own.

He looks between us and laughs. "In that case, I'm Thomas. Nice to meet you."

"Ginny," she informs him. "Arlo's cousin."

"Arlo," he repeats fondly.

Yeah, she knows my real name, Daddy. She's cool.

"What is the *meaning* of this!" My father comes storming up to us with my mother by his side. I wince, but I refuse to back down.

In fact, I stun everyone by stepping next to Thomas and letting him slip his arm around me.

My parents look like they're going to go nuclear.

"Arlington?" my mother spits.

"My name is Arlo," I tell her, shaking but determined not to back down. "And this…this is my date."

My mother splutters out a laugh and looks around at all the guests. Interestingly, Maryanne fucking Sibson is so invested in this situation, she's nowhere to be seen.

"Don't be silly, Arlington. This is…um…I mean…"

"Sir, you are trespassing," my father snarls.

Thomas shrugs, and if possible, my heart really does detonate.

He's not afraid of my parents.

"Sorry about that, Mr. Hythe-Wandsworth. But I was worried about my boyfriend here. I don't think he's been very happy since he came back from his trip."

Ginny stifles a scream, but only just. I don't blame her. *Boyfriend?* I had no idea one word could make me so delirious. My mother isn't so fortunate. Her scream is also not the happy kind. "Don't be so vulgar, young man. My son is just about to get engaged—"

"Oh, Mummy, *enough!*" I explode.

It's loud enough that it does actually render her mute. In fact, everyone is now silently staring at me.

Good.

"I'm gay," I say for the first time in my life to my parents. "I've known I was gay since I was seven years old, and if you're honest with yourself, so did you. I refuse to stay closeted in front of all these people just to make you happy. Everybody, are you listening? *I! Am! Gay!* Arlington Hythe-Wandsworth is as gay as a Christmas tree! Did everybody hear that?"

My mother looks like she's going to faint. My father has

his disappointed face on. All I care about is that Thomas hugs me tightly to him, and Ginny punches the air with a "Yesss!"

"I'm so proud of you," Thomas says.

"Fine," my father bites out. "This is all very adorable. What was your plan after this little stunt, Mr. ...?"

"Beltran," Ginny provides with great enthusiasm. "Thomas Beltran, the multi-millionaire ex-hockey player. And Arlo's his boyfriend. Mr. Beltran's fans are going to *adore* him. Isn't that right, Mr. Beltran?"

Thomas grins at my ridiculous cousin. "If Arlo is comfortable going public, I know they're going to be obsessed with him. But only if that's what he wants."

I turn to see him looking at me with such love it snatches my breath away. "I want to be with you so loudly and proudly," I tell him, my voice catching with emotion. "I'm done living this false life. I want to be with you and be *real.*"

"Young man," my father snaps. I look at him, tall, slim, gray, and pinched. Joyless. I don't know why I've been afraid of him all this time. "You have responsibilities. Whatever you're thinking, you can't just walk away from this family or our company."

Something wholly reckless sweeps over me like a wave from the beach in Bali.

"And what would you do about it if I got on this helicopter and never came back?" I ask, genuinely curious.

A gasp sweeps through the crowd.

Both my parents' mouths drop open. "You'd be penniless," my mother eventually manages to utter.

Wow. Of course that's all she can say. Not that she'd miss me or that she loves me enough to change her mind. It hurts, but it's not surprising.

Thomas barks out a laugh. He looks at me before tenderly kissing the top of my head. Then he looks at my parents.

"With all due respect, ma'am, he really, *really* wouldn't be penniless."

"I want to go with you," I blurt. It all seems crystal clear to me now.

"Of course, Arlo," Thomas says. I can tell he wants to call me Lolo, but that can come later.

We have all the time in the world for that.

I can also tell that he doesn't understand me.

I shake my head. "Not for the evening, not for a visit. I…I want to go back with you to New York. Indefinitely. I want to try living near you and dating you and starting a new life all of my own. There's nothing for me here." Horror grips me and I jerk my head to look at Ginny. "Except you, of course!"

She looks at me like I might be clinically insane. "What are you talking about? Fuck *off* out of here! If I miss you, I'll come to New York City because that really is *not* a chore. Hell. Get in this contraption right now, and I will go shove all your shit into bags and ship it to you. Do you hear me?"

I smile weakly at her. "Yes, ma'am." Then I look at Thomas. "Is that okay with you?"

He shakes his head, and for a heart-stopping moment, I worry I've really fucked everything up.

"You're not going to live *near* me, baby. You're going to live *with* me. If that's okay, then we can leave right now."

The tears I was fighting back spill as I half sob, half laugh, and kiss him in front of everyone, my parents be damned. "Let's go," I whisper.

"Wait!" Ginny throws up her hand to stop us from boarding the helicopter. "One final thought."

I stare at her and eventually give into her dramatics. "Yes?" I prompt.

She grins like the cat that found the cream. "They can't marry you off if you're already married. Just an idea." She downs her Champagne then launches into a sprint, possibly going to my bedroom to pack my stuff before anyone stops her. "I'll courier your passport tomorrow!" she yells as she disappears into the darkness.

But I'm too much in shock to really process that, turning to look at Thomas. "I mean…she's got a point. And it might help with US citizenship?"

"Is that your way of asking for another passport to lose?" Thomas asks, but he's tearful too, showing how not-crazy he thinks this idea is. He kisses the back of my hand, then leads me toward the helicopter.

"Arlington Hythe-Wandsworth!" my mother screams.

I glance over my shoulder.

"That's not my name," I say without much emotion. "Good-bye, Mummy. Good-bye, Pa. Take care of yourselves."

I step up into the helicopter and into the next chapter of my life. Thomas yells something at the pilot, and the blades start whirring again. The throng on the grass immediately step backward, giving us room.

I'm safe.

I've escaped.

It doesn't seem real, but as Thomas gently settles a headset on me, I know it to be true.

Whatever Ginny manages to pack and send, I'll appreciate. And after all the trouble it caused, I'll definitely need my passport, especially if I really do want to go to America. But honestly? I have my phone in my pocket, and everything else can be replaced.

I show Thomas the other item I have in my pocket. The only thing that couldn't be replaced and the thing I value even more than my phone.

The magnet. "You were always with me," I tell him.

He hugs me tightly as we slowly start to lift off the ground. He shoves the door so it slams shut, safely encasing us inside. "You were always with me, too, Lolo," he says, his voice coming through the headset as he rubs his chest over his heart.

"Where are we going?" I ask as we rise higher. I know a helicopter could barely get us to London, let alone New York.

He grins at me and waggles his eyebrows. "I booked us a suit at a fancy country hotel. Something told me your folks wouldn't invite me over for a slumber party."

I snort before slapping my hand against my mouth. "I can't believe that just happened," I say in awe.

"Baby boy?" Thomas says, a slightly serious tone to his voice. He rests his hand on a box on the bench we're sitting on. I didn't notice it before. It's got a grate at the front of it and a handle on top. "I got you a present."

Confused, I lean over and peer inside the box, not really understanding what I'm seeing. "You got me...a tiny lion?" The creature has a furry face and paws, but the rest of their body is shaved down to the skin. Even their tail only has a fluffy pom pom tip at the end.

Thomas laughs, then opens up the top of the box so I can see clearly inside. It *is* a tiny lion. They look up at me, meow, and...

"OH MY FUCKING GOD, IT'S JOLLY!" I scream so loudly the helicopter dips ever so slightly. I'm sure the pilot is pretending that nothing happened as he rights us again, but I'm too busy grabbing my poor naked kitty up and hugging him against my chest. "What? How?"

Thomas leans forward to wipe away the tears that are already streaming down my cheeks. "He's been on an adventure of his own," he says, clearly very pleased with himself. "Kirana was positively gleeful to help me catch him and take him to a vet. He gave him a checkup. His mats were just too bad, so we decided to shave him, but his fur should grow back pretty quickly. Other than that, he's actually in great health! One of Kirana's friends very kindly agreed to accompany him on a plane to London if I paid for the ticket. He's got a pet passport, and we'll need to top up his jabs after quarantine but…"

He sighs and cups the side of my face with his big hand. "Is he ours?" I whisper, not daring to really believe it.

"We're a crew," Thomas says thickly. "A captain doesn't leave any crew member behind."

I cry into what's left of Jolly's fur around his neck. He's looking like once we get back on solid ground again, he's going to murder every single one of us, but I don't care.

"I love you so much," I tell my angry cat. But then I look up and meet my Daddy's eyes before taking his hand in mine. "I love you *so* much," I tell him, too.

"Lolo," he says, his voice cracking. "My baby boy. Do you really want to come live with me?"

I nod. "More than anything, Daddy."

He leans over, careful of Jolly, and kisses my forehead. "I love you, too, baby boy. Here's to the start of our next adventure," he says.

I link our fingers and think about what Ginny said. I know she was joking, but my parents really *couldn't* marry me off if I were bound to someone else.

Legally, that is.

My heart is already his. It has been since I sat down across from him in that airport lounge.

But I wouldn't mind a fancy ring to prove it.

CHAPTER 21

Thomas

WELL, THAT WENT BETTER THAN I EVER COULD HAVE imagined. Still, I can't quite believe Arlo is here, that he's coming home with me. I thought I'd crash the party and declare my love for him, and then I hoped we'd come back to the hotel to spend the night. My plan was to talk in the morning about the logistics of moving our relationship forward.

Now it's going to be spent researching what kind of visa would suit him best.

My heart thumps in my chest going over what Arlo's cousin said. I wouldn't want anyone to think any marriage between us was for a green card. I'd hate to get investigated or treated like our relationship was a scam.

But it *would* make several things a whole lot easier. Besides, the romantic in me just really like the idea.

Mama was right. It doesn't matter if it's two weeks or two years. I know this boy is the one. He completes me like a missing puzzle piece I didn't even know wasn't there. He is my sunshine, my oxygen. And it was *his* idea to move stateside, so that just makes me even more confident.

I'll always look to him to make sure the relationship is on course. He's the real captain of this crew. So the fact that he came up with this plan all on his own makes me want to burst with happiness.

My boy wants me. I feel like my crush just invited me to the prom—something that of course never happened to me back in school.

When my injury ended my playing career in an instant, I was forced to reevaluate everything and try to keep positive, seeing the changes as a new beginning, the second chapter of my life. And yeah, I do love my work now and absolutely still have purpose.

But *this* feels like the true second beginning. Until now, I've viewed my life in two halves: hockey and no hockey. But the truth is that I'll always have the sport I love from all the kids I coach and support. Seeing them live their dreams fulfills me in a completely different way than I felt being on the ice myself.

Now, my life will be divided into before Arlo and after he came into my life.

The country hotel has a helipad on the roof. It's the main reason why I picked it. The more wine my sister and I consumed the other night, the wilder my scheme became. But when I woke up slightly hungover the next day, I refused to back down from any of the madness. Camila had said I needed to go big or go home, so that's what I did.

And now I'm going home with my boy.

We manage to get a very unhappy Jolly back into his box as we begin our descent. The hotel is also pet-friendly. I thought finding something that fit all my requirements in a close enough proximity to Arlo's parents' house would be impossible, but I guess it shows what kinds of people live in this part of England as it was shockingly easy.

Once we touch down and the blades slowly stop spinning, I thank the pilot for joining me on my harebrained scheme, remove my and Arlo's headsets, then open up the door for us.

"Mind your step," I warn my baby boy, holding his hand as he carefully gets out.

"Thank you, Daddy," he says warmly. As soon as he's on solid ground, he reaches back in the chopper and retrieves Jolly in his box. He takes a deep breath and looks up at the night sky. "We're free," he says, his voice catching a little.

I touch his chin with my finger and thumb, gently encouraging him to look back down at me so I can kiss him softly on the lips. "We're free," I agree.

I know we're both mostly talking about the constraints of his overbearing parents and everything they expected of him. But I also feel free of all the pressure I put on myself. I was so afraid that I'd never be able to find the kind of relationship I wanted that I didn't even try and search for it.

It's a good thing I didn't, really. Otherwise, I would probably have never met my perfect boy. But still, I'm relieved that I don't have that fear I put on myself that I'd never find love and always be lonely when I came home at night.

In a matter of weeks, I've gone from being a sad bachelor to having my own family. I couldn't ask for anything more if I tried.

We make our way down the fire escape stairs that lead from the roof to the lobby. After we walk through the door, I take Arlo's hand, threading our fingers together. He grips onto Jolly's carry case with his other hand, and I appreciate this is all he owns in the world right now.

Arlo already messaged Ginny so she can mail whatever she can to my place in New York. She's promised that she'll get his passport here tomorrow as well as his special stuffies, Chippy and Snap. He almost got distressed when he realized he'd left them behind, but Ginny sent him a photo to assure him that she'd already rescued them. Apparently, in the end nobody stopped her from ransacking Arlo's room. The sad truth is that they didn't seem to care.

Bastards.

I look at him now and can't wrap my head around the idea that anyone could not love him. Well, I've got more than enough love to make up for all those assholes.

He looks handsome in his tuxedo, but I'll need to order him some clothes for the next few days. The idea of dressing my boy fills me with a pleasure I've never known before. This goes way beyond when I bought the few bits for my vacation, like the beach toys. Those were for a hypothetical boy.

Anything I purchase now will specifically be for *Arlo*. I'll get him jeans and underwear and stuff, but I wonder what I can also buy with pirates and mermaids and sea creatures on them. Even when he's not being little, I bet he'll enjoy a range of fun T-shirts to wear.

He doesn't have to ever worry about being a 'real grown-up man' ever again. With me, he can always feel free to show his joy and his passions. That's why I love him.

And he loves me, I remember in a flash of happiness. We said it out loud. It's true.

I really have hit the jackpot.

The front desk is staffed twenty-four seven, so there's a young man waiting for us there as we approach. "Hello, Mr. Beltran," he says cheerfully despite the hour.

It doesn't matter how much I travel or how much good customer service I'm privileged to receive. I always get a kick out of people taking the time to make their guests feel extra welcome.

"This must be your friend you mentioned, Mr. Hythe-Wandsworth?"

I wince, realizing that actually in this case, committing

our names to memory might not have the desired result. Arlo hates his name so much. But when I look down, my boy is beaming.

"Not for much longer," he says cheekily, winking at me. In that moment, I realize something. Who cares if our marriage-of-convenience chat was just hot air to piss off his folks? The idea of him taking my name gives me such a rush that it doesn't matter if it's next week or in ten years' time.

Arlo Beltran has a fucking awesome ring to it.

The receptionist touches his chest and gasps. "Is that so?" he coos. "Congratulations, both of you. If you don't mind me saying, you make a very handsome couple."

I wrap my arm around Arlo and hug him to my side. "We don't mind you saying at all, sir."

The guy beams at us, then raises his eyebrows. "You're all checked in, Mr. Beltran, and I believe I gave you two key cards earlier. Is there anything else I can help you with?"

I squeeze Arlo's side. "My sister made me pack a toothbrush for you, just in case. Is there anything else you need? Are you hungry?"

"The kitchen is still open for another couple of hours," the receptionist assures us happily.

Arlo suddenly looks very tired, but he smiles. "Food sounds great, actually. And I wouldn't mind borrowing a phone charger if you have one."

"Of course," the guy says. They quickly work out what cable matches his model, and then he shows us a menu from the restaurant. "This has everything, unlike the room service menu," he tells us with a wink. "We can accommodate something special for you gentlemen, though."

He bustles away to occupy himself on the computer while we look at the options. "What do you want, baby boy?" I whisper in his ear.

"You," he says with a giggle. "But also chips. By which I mean fries, not crisps."

I kiss his hair. "I know, sweetheart. I'm learning to speak your weird language."

"I think you'll find that *England* invented *English,*" he says with an adorable huff.

We both end up ordering fries, except I think chips might actually be the better word as apparently, they're chunky, triple-cooked, and with the skin on, or so the guy explains to us. Potato is potato to me. I get a steak, and Arlo gets a chicken pie, and we both get chocolate cake to share.

Proper comfort food.

"Does Jolly have things in the room?" Arlo asks before we leave the desk.

"Mr. Beltran organized the full pet package, Mr. Hythe-Wandsworth," the guy assures him. "If your furry friend needs anything else, please call down and let me know."

"We will," I tell him, then look down at Arlo, still snug against me, wrapped tightly in my arm. "Ready?"

"Yes, D—" He blushes and swallows the word, although I don't think our friend here would judge us if he called me 'Daddy,' and my hearts swells regardless. "Yes, I'm ready."

"Then let's head up." I nod at the guy. "Thank you for everything."

"My pleasure," he says warmly.

I know the UK isn't super hot on tipping, but I'm still going to leave a big cash envelope for him when we leave anyway. After Arlo was treated so cruelly by his parents, the fact that the very next human being we met was so kind and supportive of him makes such a difference.

The hotel is a former family estate, probably quite similar to Arlo's home we just left behind. The cream walls, the large painted portraits hanging from them, the crystal chandeliers, and sweeping staircase all remind me of the regency romance novels my sister kept mentioning all throughout our brainstorming session. She wanted drama from my excursion, and boy, did we get it. I can't wait to tell her all about it.

Ours is the biggest room in the place—another minor miracle, considering how late I made the booking. We have a living room area as well as our bedroom and a large bathroom. I know we have to wait for our food, but once we've released Jolly so he can shoot under the sofa to hide, I make short work of stripping my baby's fancy suit off until he's down to his boxer-briefs, then I wrap him in a fluffy complimentary robe.

As I do the same, hanging our clothes in the wardrobe and putting my hat back in its box and placing Arlo's baseball cap on top of it, Arlo nips around me and fishes a couple of things from his pants pockets.

His phone and the magnet.

"Just going to text Ginny," he says, clutching the magnet to his chest like a protective talisman.

He won't need that when we get to New York. Everything will be his, and everything will remind him that he's mine and that he's loved.

Our food doesn't take long to arrive, and I discover that the TV actually has its own streaming service with a range of media available, like airplane entertainment. I let Arlo pick an animated film that I only half pay attention to as we eat.

Mostly, I just watch him relaxing and having fun, feeling content to my bones.

As it's a kids' movie, it's not very long, which is good because after being separated for two weeks, I need Arlo naked and pressed against me like yesterday. Still, I want this to be special, so I don't jump him as soon as the credits roll.

Instead, I let him have some time with Jolly, feeding him leftover steak and chicken and laughing gently about his drastic haircut. "Don't worry," I hear him promising the cat as I move to the bathroom. "It won't take long for it to all grow back. I'm going to brush you every single day so any mats you get will quickly be taken care of."

I'm not sure Jolly is convinced, but he'll soon get used to the new order of things. Knowing my boy's heart is mended because Kirana helped us adopt him is one of the greatest gifts I could ever imagine.

The bathroom is so big it actually has a big clawfoot copper tub. The outside is a pretty marbled teal color that matches the shade of all the complimentary products. I pour bubble bath into the water that's running, the scent of jasmine quickly filling the air. There's even a sachet of scented flower petals to scatter on the surface which I do, because why the hell not?

"Baby boy?" I call him in once the tub is half-full. He comes scampering through the door, grinning as his robe accidentally on purpose falls open.

"Yes, Daddy?"

I hum, taking the robe off all the way and hanging it on the heated rail. Then I slip his underwear off, give him my hand, and help him into the water. He looks up at me, surrounded by bubbles and floating flower petals, and my breath catches.

"You are so beautiful," I murmur.

He blushes and looks away for a second before biting his lip and meeting my gaze again. "So are you, Daddy. Are you going to get in, too?"

Wild fucking horses couldn't hold me back. "Of course," I say, quickly putting my robe with his and dropping my briefs to the floor. I kick them away before slipping into the water behind him, wrapping my arms and legs around his sweet body, trapping him because he's mine.

He squirms against me and moans. "Daddy," he whines, making me laugh.

"Does my naughty little slut want something?" I ask.

He looks over his shoulder at me and pouts. "I've been terribly good," he protests.

I arch an eyebrow. "Are you telling me that you haven't touched yourself since Bali?"

He snorts. "No, Daddy. I've wanked off every single night, thinking about you."

My laugh is loud, but I soon silence myself by kissing his pretty lips. "Such a potty mouth," I mumble. "I'll have to think of ways to keep it quiet."

He sucks in a breath as my hand envelopes his hardening cock, stroking it in the water, kissing him as he trembles. But then he suddenly turns around, sloshing water over the edge. It's a good thing I only half filled the tub, as with both of us in here it got pretty full, and now he's giving me his best impression of a killer whale in a goldfish bowl.

I forget all about the water, however, when he straddles me and lines our cocks up, stroking us together. I groan and wrap my hand around his so we work together. His dick feels so perfect against mine. It doesn't take long before we're both spilling into the water.

I'm glad I booked us a few days in the hotel. I wasn't sure what we'd be doing, so I haven't booked any flights back to New York yet. But that means I can spend the next couple of days doing nothing but fucking my incredible, sweet, perfect boy in every way I can imagine pleasuring him.

For now, sharing an orgasm in the tub seems like the perfect way to finish our wild evening. I kiss him softly while we come down, then I drag myself out of the water to get our towels, drying us both off, ready to sleep.

As I haul him under the covers, I sigh and wrap my limbs around him again like an octopus. This time, he's facing me, and he giggles as he lays his head on my chest. "I missed you," he admits in the dark.

I chuckle ruefully. "I haven't had a decent night's sleep since Bali."

That night, though, I sleep like a log, safe in the knowledge that everything I need in the world is all in this room. I've got my crew. I've got my love.

Who knows what adventures the high seas will bring us next? All I know is that Arlo was right. We're free men, now. We get to live our lives the way we choose.

Together.

Epilogue – One Year Later

Arlo

Laughter fills the air, along with the delicious smells coming from the barbecue. Kids run around, chasing each other with little water pistols, and music pulses from the speakers set up in several places. I sit at a folding table with a baby on my lap, trying not to become overwhelmed by all the love I feel.

Thomas has a big, noisy family that I adore. So many cousins, uncles, and aunties and women who apparently aren't related to anyone, but we call them auntie anyway. Everybody talks to me and asks about my work at Thomas's foundation. I love the genuine passion that wells up every time I talk about working with the kids and giving back to the community.

Who knew that work could be something to enjoy and be proud of? It's crazy how different my life is compared to just last year. And it's all thanks to Thomas.

My husband.

Apparently, neither of us wanted to talk the other out of it, and we did end up legally marrying only a couple of months after I moved to America. It just made everything easier for me to stay, and it closed a door with my parents for good. This isn't the 1800s and I doubt they really could have married me off. It was more metaphorical than that. It was me telling them that they don't have any control over me anymore, and if they want to be a part of my life, they have to find a way to accept and respect me.

So far, I haven't heard anything back from them, and that's okay. I don't want to have a relationship with them if they're not going to change. But they know where I am if they ever do want to reach out.

In the meantime, I look around the roof of our building that Thomas booked out for the day, seeing so many happy people smiling, eating, and drinking.

My name is Arlo Beltran, and I belong here.

I'm still getting used to the culture shock of moving to a big city after all my sheltered rural living. Thomas is still a little terrified about letting me use the subway by myself. But together we're both learning that I'm tougher than I seem and can handle a lot more than I ever thought possible.

New Yorkers can be frighteningly loud and argumentative, but it's authentic in a way that I deeply appreciate. I feel like the people I work with and I see in my everyday life are more genuine than the circles I used to move in around my parents. I'll take a feisty cab driver or a noisy bar of sports fans over the mind games that come from stony silences any day of the week.

And then there's my work. It's so hands on. The only options presented to me for employment until now were sitting on boards, going to meetings, and shuffling money and emails around. I know I would have really hated it. Now, I split my time organizing travel for the kids in Thomas's hockey program and working at a local daycare his foundation sponsors. I sit with toddlers on my lap as they fingerpaint and stop them from pushing lollipop sticks up their noses. It's messy and chaotic and I couldn't love it more.

Thomas's mum reminds me about once a month that gay couples can have babies, too. Often, his sister, Camila, comes to my rescue, but I really don't mind it.

My parents would remind me that it was my duty to produce an heir. Thomas's mama gets starry-eyed and talks softly about how much she'd love grandbabies. It makes me think about having children in ways I never have before. I know I'll always be Thomas's baby boy. But we have room in our hearts for love beyond ourselves, I'm sure.

As proven when Thomas came home in the rain one day with a shivering gray tabby kitten bundled up in his coat. We looked around to see if anyone reported her missing, but when the vet said she wasn't microchipped, we pretty much adopted her straight away. I was worried how Jolly might react to Zheng Yi Sao joining our crew, but it turned out he absolutely loved having a little minion trailing him around, learning all his tricks.

The two of them are currently downstairs in our apartment, away from the chaos of such a large family gathering, probably plotting world domination. I send regular updates to Kirana as we soon became friends on Insta after I moved. She calls the cats her babies and always asks after them before me or Thomas. I'm looking forward to seeing her when we fly back to Bali in a couple of weeks to celebrate our one-year anniversary.

I would never have dared to think my life could be so perfect, but as I look across the crowded roof at my husband, I take a breath and remember that I'm a good person who deserves good things.

Thomas glances over and catches me looking at him, a grin spreading over his face. He reaches down to one of the tables and grabs a spoon, tapping it to the beer bottle in his hand. "Hey, guys," he yells out.

Someone turns the music down. Another person gently takes the baby from my lap with a wink, so I rise to my feet to go stand by my Daddy.

When he has the group's attention, he puts the spoon down, wrapping his free arm around me, and raising his drink up in a toast. "Thank you all so much for coming. For some of you, this is the first chance you've had to meet my partner, Arlo." I blush as several people whoop and cheer, but I do love how loud they are with their approval of me. "As you probably know, we got married last year for several different legal reasons. But…it wasn't especially romantic."

He glances at me, and my stomach swoops. What's he doing?

I watch as he places his bottle on a nearby table…then gets down on one knee.

I blink as people scream and gasp. "Darling," I say in confusion. "We're already married."

He jerks a thumb over his shoulder. "You think I was going to get away with stopping this pack of wolves from throwing a party?" He reaches into his pocket and laughs. "Besides, I didn't get to do *this*. And, baby, you deserve everything."

The box in his hand is lined with black velvet. He opens it to reveal a rose gold band inside. I peer closer to make out the details on it.

"It's a compass," I whisper in awe.

He nods. "So you'll always be able to find your way home to my love."

I sniff, momentarily frozen, unable to comprehend how my life could possibly get any better right now.

"Arlo!" Mama cries in frustration. "Is that a yes?"

It's all ridiculous. We're already married, for heaven's

sake. But I still burst into tears as I nod. "Yes," I splutter. The entire rooftop goes wild, cheering, clapping, whistling, banging cutlery on crockery, the works. My parents would deem it completely uncouth, and that's what makes it so bloody perfect.

"Wedding!" Camila is yelling at the top of her lungs over the New York skyline. "My baby brother is getting hitched, y'all!" One of the aunties pops a bottle of Champagne that's appeared from nowhere. In fact, there seems to be a lot of Champagne all of a sudden. Then people are pulling party poppers, sending streamers flying through the air.

I turn and look at Thomas. "Welcome to your engagement party," he says to me. I laugh and kiss him on the lips, but then he looks thoughtful. "If only we had some CAKE," he shouts. I flinch, no idea why he'd do that when I'm literally so close I'm in his arms. But his uncle Leo opens the roof door with a flourish, and out steps…

"GINNY!" I cry, more tears immediately falling from my eyes.

"I told you I'd come visit," she crows, sashaying toward us with a huge cake in her hands. It's got sparklers crackling all over it, but underneath the lights, I can see all the little pirate ships and mermaids and parrots. I love that Thomas doesn't make me try and hide the things I love in front of other people.

"Matelotage," Thomas whispers in my ear.

I nod at him. "I'll marry you on all the seven seas if you like."

He grins. "You're on."

Once the sparklers fade out, Mama takes it upon herself to start cutting the cake and sharing it out. I watch as Camila introduces herself to Ginny, both women grinning like maniacs.

"Should we be worried about that?" I ask.

"Absolutely," Thomas replies.

"Is there any way to stop them?"

"Nope!" Thomas says, laughing and kissing my neck.

This is my family. My big, messy, chaotic family, full of fun and games and most importantly…love and respect. This is where I belong.

With my Daddy at the top of the world.

———

Thank you so much for reading **Arlo and Thomas's** story! If you enjoyed their summer adventure, please leave a review on your favorite bookish site. It makes a big difference for us indie authors!

Have you read all the other books in the **A Daddy For Summer** series? Make sure you don't miss a single one of these delightful stories that readers have been raving about **here**!

Want to see how Andreas, Jalen and Colby got together? You can read their **A Daddy For Christmas** book **here**!

Turn the page to discover more heartwarming Daddy books by Helen Juliet/HJ Welch.

———

Thank you to my team!

Cover Design: Jo Clement

Editing: Meg Cooper

Proof Reading: Tanja Ongkiehong

Love and support: Ed, AK, Jodi, Hubby and our cats

Also Available

A Daddy For Christmas (multi-author shared universe): Jalen & Colby by HJ Welch

One Daddy, two boys, and the epic road trip that brings them together

ANDREAS

While selling a bunch of stuff that's been sitting in storage here in Sydney, I end up with two guys aggressively bidding on the same childhood toy. I worry I've got a fight on my hands until I realize they're actually best friends trying to buy it for each other as a Christmas gift. The solution? Simple! They live right here in the city, so I hand deliver the present for both of them to share. What's not so simple is how adorable these young men are. How gorgeous. How the more time we spend together, the more it's starting to feel like love…

JALEN

Of course I love my BFF, Colby. Duh. I moved from California to Australia for him! But I know as much as I want him to be mine, I'm a walking disaster and he needs someone better than me to take care of him. Someone like Andreas. He appears in our life like a Christmas miracle, looking after both of us like some sort of dream Daddy. It doesn't hurt that he's not only successful but crazy generous. He seems to adore spoiling us, so when he offers to take us on an amazing trip back to his home in the UK for the holidays, how can we refuse? And if we just happen to accidentally fall into bed together, would that be so terrible?

COLBY

Thanks to the power of the internet, Jalen has been there for me for years when my own family turned their backs on me. But even after we move in together, I know he just sees me as a friend. He's too fabulous, too bright and beautiful for shy little me, so I've never said a word. However, something strange starts happening the more time we spend with our new friend, Andreas. The older man gives the most amazing cuddles and can't seem to stop showering me and Jalen with gifts. Traveling to England feels like something from a fairy tale, but what's even more unbelievable is the way his eyes light up when he's with me and my best friend. Am I crazy? Could three really be the magic number?

Jalen & Colby is part of A Daddy for Christmas, a multi-author series. *All the books are standalones, but each Daddy has a unique gift for his wonderful boy (or boys). Except all boys know that sometimes Santa gets it wrong, and it's going to take a very special Daddy to make it right. So why not stay and read them all?*

Click here to get the Jalen & Colby eBook

Also Available

Daddy's Fairy Tales Box Set by Helen Juliet

Experience Goldilocks and the Three Bears, Little Red Riding Hood, The Three Little Pigs, and Puss in Boots as you've never seen them before in this box set of contemporary adaptations! Available together for the first time, each stand alone book features a caring Daddy finding his HEA with a loving boy (or boys!)

Golden

When Goldie's ex-boyfriend leaves him in serious debt with the adult entertainment company he works for, Goldie gets the chance to work off the money…in front of the camera. The idea excites him, but then his favourite throuple—Daddy, Papa, and Baby—*demand* he comes to play with them. No matter how scared he is, he can't miss this opportunity, not even when his past comes back to haunt him.

Wild Ride

When Red is chased into the woods, he seeks sanctuary at his estranged grandma's house. He doesn't expect to be rescued by his older brother's best friend, the man he was always madly in love with. Could Hunter be the Daddy of Red's wildest dreams? Especially when he unlocks a secret passion of Red's for beautiful lingerie. There's still a threat lurking in the woods, though, and Hunter realises he'll do anything to protect his beautiful boy.

Three

When three shy best friends sign up to a dating app to finally get some by the end of the year, they don't expect to all fall for the same

gorgeous, slightly scary-looking Daddy. The only solution? Let him choose who he wants to bed. Except he doesn't. Daddy Wolf wants to spoil each little piggy, one after another. But when danger comes calling, will their love for each other be enough to save them all?
Includes Halloween bonus scene!

Nine Lives

When Charlie suddenly finds himself homeless and penniless, he decides to sell the only thing left he owns. Himself. For the very first time. Lucky for him he stumbles across Miller, the own of a London kink club, who saves him from those who would take advantage of him. As Miller discovers his inner Daddy, he also unlocks Charlie's kitten alter-ego. But with both their families meddling, will new love be enough to keep them together?

Click here to get the Daddy's Fairy Tales Box Set

Paddle Creek Daddies #1: Heaven Sent by HJ Welch

Two rival jocks. One adorable nerd. A bet that changes everything.

SETH

Being captain of the Paddle Creek Panthers is my life. I wouldn't care that my grades have slipped, except it could not only cost me my shot at the pros, but now the rich kid in town has wagered that if I don't graduate, I'll owe him *big* time. Can this gorgeous little freshman geek Gabe really save my degree and my reputation? All I know is that as soon as I laid eyes on him, I needed him. And I *don't* want to share.

MARTY

I've spent almost four years trying to get my captain Seth to notice me. He's hot as hell and knows how to boss a guy around, even one as big as me. To him, though, I'm just the team clown. But when he drags me into this graduation bet, it's no laughing matter. So why shouldn't this little cherub Gabe tutor me as well? In fact, I don't see why we can't share him in all *kinds* of ways. Seth is clearly a natural Daddy, Gabe thrives being doted on, and I'm happy to Daddy *and* be Daddied. Win-win, right?

GABE

Somehow, I've found myself standing up to the guy whose family pretty much owns Paddle Creek and put my neck on the line for two of the college's star players. Now we're spending every day together as I try and save their grades, and I don't know if I'm crazy but it's like they both *want* me. I've never had a boyfriend. I'm not even out to my overbearing parents. How could I choose between them…or do I actually have to when they *both* want to be my Daddies? After my life comes crashing down, it's their turn to come to my rescue. Maybe what me and these god-like men have isn't just a fling after all?

*Heaven Sent is a steamy, standalone MMM romance. It's the first book in the **Paddle Creek Daddies** series, where it's always the quiet ones who get up to the best kind of trouble. This book features a geek tutoring two hot jocks, two hot jocks tutoring a geek in a completely different way, a trash panda with a heart of gold, a human ice cream sundae, a revenge curse, and a guaranteed HEA with absolutely no cliffhanger.*

Click here to get the Heaven Sent eBook

Also Available

Paddle Creek Daddies #2: Yes, Sir by HJ Welch

Two men. Two secrets. Can true love set them free?

BENEDICT

Just one more year, then I can go back to my beloved Oxford University and leave this tiny town behind me. Teaching is my passion, but I have other desires that I know would get me fired if anyone found out. The only trouble is, my new TA is pushing all my buttons and I'm not sure he even realizes what calling me Sir does to me. That's nothing, however, compared to when he starts calling me Daddy.

JACKSON

Have I got hots for teacher? Oh, yes. Messing around is off the table, though, so in a way it's safe to flirt with him and see him lose that stiff upper lip. It's not like he'd be interested in me anyway if he ever discovered what I love wearing under my clothes. Tough guys like me shouldn't like satin and lace. They shouldn't want to feel pretty. But Sir makes me feel gorgeous, and I want to be *such* a good boy for him.

*Yes, Sir is a steamy, standalone MM romance. It's the second book in the **Paddle Creek Daddies** series, where it's always the quiet ones who get up to the best kind of trouble. This book features two people learning they don't have to be ashamed of who they are, a sassy brat who really wants to behave, a master in the bedroom who's a caring Daddy at heart, role playing so good it could win an Oscar, and a guaranteed HEA with absolutely no cliffhanger.*

Click here to get the Yes, Sir eBook

Also Available

Paddle Creek Daddies #3: Little Pleasures by HJ Welch

One jaded Daddy. One brand new boy. A fake relationship that becomes all too real.

XANDER

It's bad enough I have to move back to Paddle Creek with my awful stepmom, but now my half-brother's best friend has decided he has to look after me—even pretending to be my new boyfriend for a family wedding to keep my stepmother off my back. What Ruben doesn't know is that I've been in love with him for as long as I can remember and spending so much time with him is torture. Until it isn't. I can't believe that he's interested in me and even wants to be my Daddy, unlocking something in me I never knew was there. But when my stepmom goes too far, can I rely on Ruben to be there for me seeing as no one else in my life ever has?

RUBEN

When my life-long best friend asks me to keep an eye on his half-brother, of course I agree. Except he's a young man now, not a kid, and he's tugging at every single one of my Daddy heartstrings. Xander has just moved back into town and between finishing his degree, part-time work, and hellish stepmother, he's stressing himself into knots. It's a long time since a boy interested me, but I just want to protect Xander from the whole world. No matter the cost.

Little Pleasures is a steamy, standalone MM romance. It's the third book in the **Paddle Creek Daddies** series, where it's always the quiet ones who get up to the best kind of trouble. This book features a Daddy introducing a *boy to his inner little, the most loyal doggy best friend, a lot of dinosaurs, a heart-stopping rescue, and a guaranteed HEA with absolutely no cliffhanger. CW: Age play but no ABDL.*

Click here to get the Little Pleasures eBook

Also Available

Paddle Creek Daddies #4: Four Play by HJ Welch

Three hungry wolves. One pretty little lamb. The hunt for love is on.

HARPER

I'm here for a good time, not a long time. When a total cutie asks me if I'd be interested in him and his two Daddies chasing me down and having their way with me, it sounds fun. I'm only in this crappy town for the summer, after all. But what we share is *intense.* I signed on to get caught…not to catch feels. However, when I find myself being hunted for real, can I really expect my wolf pack to come to the rescue?

RICK

After my husband and I swapped military life for married life, we quickly met our sweet baby boy who we'll do anything for. When Brady says he's found a sassy little lamb for the three of us to stalk, I'm happy to indulge him. But this broken young man swiftly captures all of our hearts, even though he says he can walk away any time. However, there's a difference between walking and being taken. Now I have the scent of a fool who's about to discover what happens when he's stolen what's *mine.*

*Four Play is a super steamy, standalone MMMM romance. It's the fourth book in the **Paddle Creek Daddies** series, where it's always the quiet ones who get up to the best kind of trouble. This book features exhilarating primal play, one hell of a paint ball match, an underwater themed motel, so many smooches, an obsessive ex-boyfriend, and a guaranteed HEA with absolutely no cliffhanger.*

Click here to get the Four Play eBook

Also Available

Paddle Creek Daddies #5: Hell's Kitten by HJ Welch

One grumpy biker. One sunshine kitten. Could it be a purr-fect love?

JESSIE

Okay, so maaayyybbee surprising my boyfriend was a bad idea, especially since apparently he already *has* a boyfriend and it isn't me. My only option for now is to sleep in my car. That is until the big, bad, tattooed biker who owns the cat café insists on letting me stay with him. I swore off men, but the way he dotes on me has me falling for him fast. My inner kitten is out of the bag, and there's no putting him back now.

NIM

I'm a terrible Daddy. My last kitten told me that. Words and emotions are tough for me. But when the perfect boy drops into my lap, how can I refuse? Rescuing strays is what I do. It's only so long that I can resist this beautiful kitten and his bubbly personality. But someone in town has it out for me and my fellow bikers, branding us troublemakers. I can't let Jessie be dragged down with me, not when it puts everything he's worked so hard for at risk. I swore I'd do anything to protect him. Even if that means letting him go.

*Hell's Kitten is a steamy, standalone MM romance. It's the fifth book in the **Paddle Creek Daddies series**, where it's always the quiet ones who get up to the best kind of trouble. This book features first-time kitten play, two broken hearts, a cheerleading championship, far too many black cats to count, enough love for nine whole lives, and a guaranteed HEA with absolutely no cliffhanger.*

Click here to get the Hell's Kitten eBook

Also Available

Paddle Creek Daddies #6: Make Believe by HJ Welch

One scorned doll. His enemy's straight father. Is it revenge, or could this be true love?

KADENCE

Secretly fooling around with a closeted D-bag like Logan McKenna was always a bad idea. So I ended it, much to his fury. Retribution is swift, and his humiliation of me is devastating. I can't let him get away with it, though. That's why a chance meeting with his supposedly straight father seems like the perfect revenge scheme. I'll seduce him with my alter ego, Kiki the living doll, and once I have some juicy photos, I'll ruin the entire family.

Except Rafferty McKenna is nothing like his son. He's kind, thoughtful, tender, and not to mention hot as all sin. I've been broken down by not only his son but my homophobic family and my callous ex-Daddy. But as Rafferty starts to piece me back together with love and care, can I really go through with this plan of mine?

RAFFERTY

When a living doll throws himself at me, it doesn't matter that he's a boy not a girl. He's simply *mine* and I can do whatever I want with him. One passionate encounter at a party won't do, so I invite him to stay with me for a weekend, but even that's not enough. He makes me feel alive in a way my failed marriage never has. However, as our connection gets deeper, I can tell he's keeping secrets. This is just a fling, and I can't seriously be thinking about burning my whole life down for something that's not even real. Right?

__Make Believe__ is a steamy, standalone MM romance. It's the sixth book in the __Paddle Creek Daddies series__, where it's always the quiet ones who get up to the best kind of trouble. This book features Kiki the fabulous, bratty doll who will do anything for her Daddy, an extremely naughty conference call, a romantic picnic, two hearts in need of mending, plenty of secrets that need to come out, and a guaranteed HEA with absolutely no cliffhanger.

__Content warnings:__ This book features a scene of consensual sharing, as well as a loveless marriage with both husband and wife knowingly cheating on one another. However, Kadence and Rafferty never cheat on each other.

Click here to get the Make Believe eBook

About the Author

HJ Welch is a British author of contemporary American MM small town series and books in multi authored shared universes, including the international number one best-selling Homecoming Hearts. She lives just outside of London with her husband and three balls of fluff that occasionally pretend to be cats.

She began writing at an early age, later honing her craft online in the world of fanfiction on sites like Wattpad. Fifteen years and over half a million words later, she sought out original MM novels to read. By the end of 2016 she had written her first book of her own, and in 2017 she achieved her lifelong dream of becoming a full-time author.

When she's not writing she's usually dancing, singing, filming music videos, taking long walks, working on jigsaw puzzles, drinking prosecco, or talking about Eurovision.

She also writes contemporary British MM fairy tale adaptation as Helen Juliet, including bestsellers Thorn in His Side, A Right Royal Affair, and Three.

———

You can contact Helen via the following:
Newsletter: https://www.subscribepage.com/helenjuliet
Website – www.hjwelch.com
Facebook Group – Helen's Jewels
Instagram – @helenjwrites

Twitter – @helenjwrites
Book Bub – @HJWelchAuthor
Facebook Page – @HJWelchAuthor

www.ingramcontent.com/pod-product-compliance
Lightning Source LLC
Chambersburg PA
CBHW051222210726
48290CB00003B/753